THE GUINEA PIG TRILOGY

Pig Tails

The First-Ever Guinea Pig Novel

merridypugh.com & guineapigempire.com

The Guinea Pig Trilogy
Book 1: Pig Tails – The First-Ever Guinea Pig Novel

Published 2017 by merridypugh.com & guineapigempire.com
merridypugh@gmail.com
Tasmania, Australia

National Library of Australia Cataloguing-in-Publication entry

Creator: Pugh, Merridy, author.
Title: Pig tails : the first-ever guinea pig novel / Merridy Pugh.

ISBN: 9780994641205 (paperback)

Series: Pugh, Merridy, Guinea pig trilogy ; bk 1.
Subjects: Guinea pigs--Tasmania--Fiction.
Guinea pigs--Behavior--Fiction.
Orphanages--Tasmania--Fiction.

Printed and bound by IngramSpark, Lightning Source Inc.

Cover design, illustrations and book design: Merridy Anne Pugh
Cover photograph: Merridy Anne Pugh

THE GUINEA PIG TRILOGY

BOOK 1

Pig Tails

The First-Ever Guinea Pig Novel

BY MERRIDY PUGH

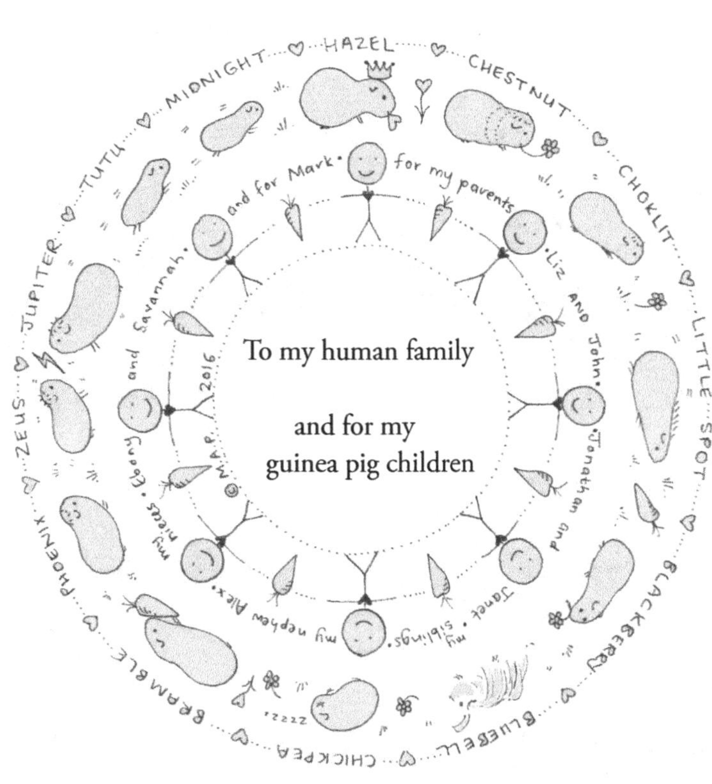

To my human family

and for my guinea pig children

'*Pig Tails* opens a window onto the realm of *guinea piggus domesticus*, a species highly underrated by the world at large but destined to become humanity's most sought after furry companion.' – *HHH*

'A gentle tale, with a dash of dry humour and a pinch of pathos. You'll never see a guinea pig with the same eyes again.' – *TRC*

'*Pig Tails* gave me a new respect for guinea pigs. Hazel One-Eye is irresistible.' – *LMGPE*

'A domestic tale with cosmic implications. I can't wait for Books Two and Three!' – *HB*

'This deceptively simple story holds lightly an exploration of the ageless subjects of life, death, love and connection. *Pig Tails* is written with a deep affection, a delightful play on words, and the clear sight of the wise.' – *EHOE*

Author's Note: I'm embarrassed to say that His Highness Hazel, The Royal Cream, Lord and Master of the Guinea Pig Empire (etc) concocted these review statements and forced me to put them in a prominent position. They are quite true of course, but one should not blow one's own trumpet.

Disclaimer

Pig Tails is a work of fiction. The guinea pig characters are based on real guinea pigs but the events of the story are fictional, that is to say, made up. Although, if you have spotted a one-eyed Pig God hovering in the stratosphere, please notify me at once.

The human characters are entirely fictitious, barring my human family who kindly allowed me to use their names and persons, but whose characters I embellished for the purposes of the story. The character who bears my name has also been altered for the purposes of the story, including her thoughts, words and actions. All other resemblance to persons living or dead is coincidental.

Hobart is a real place. So is Tasmania. The weather is accurately described.

Merridy Anne Pugh, 2017, Hobart

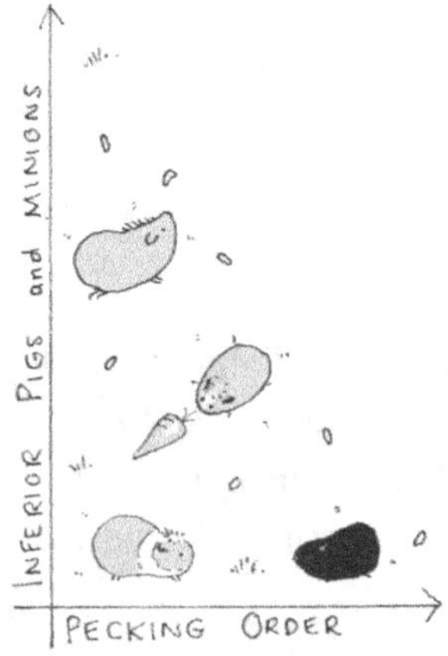

Hazel's Island Kingdom

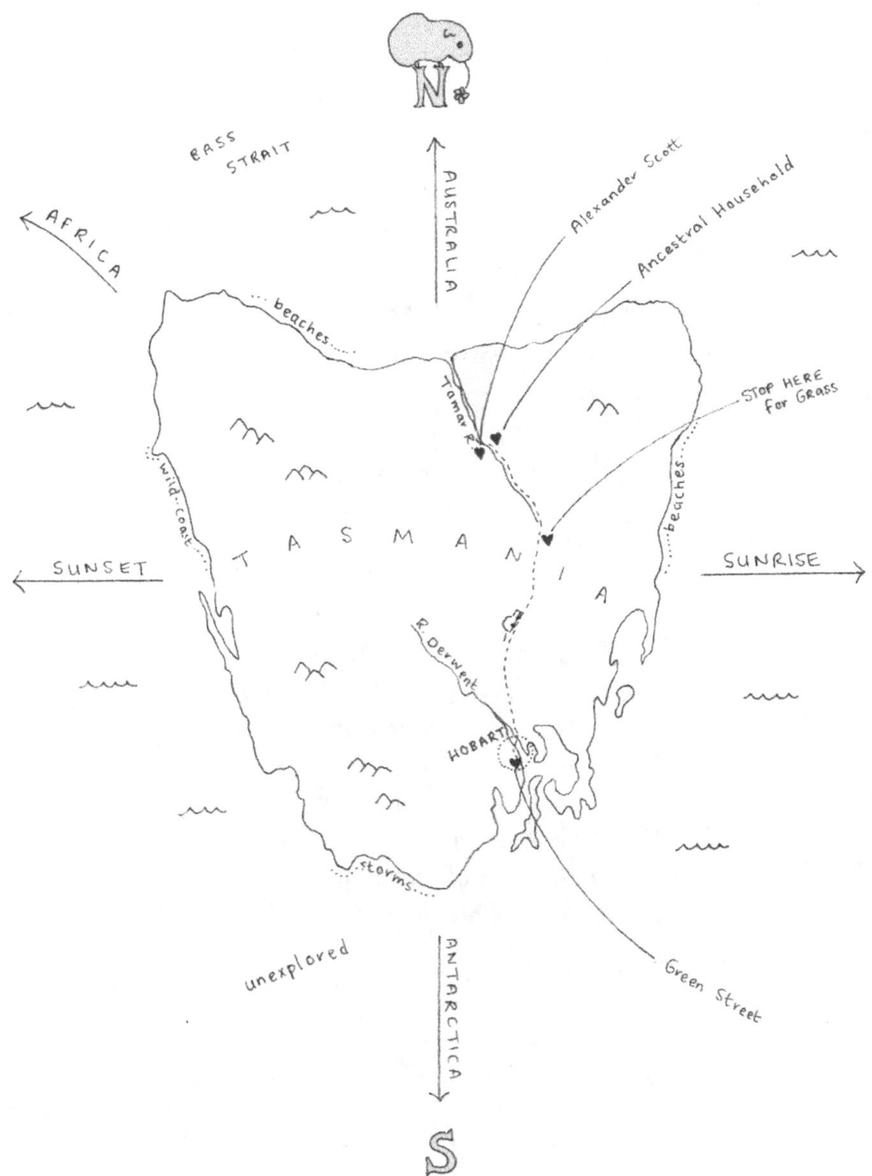

CONTENTS

Part two • The wounded emperor

Ebony: 'But guinea pigs have no tails.'

Guinea pig mother: 'I know. But they have plenty of stories. It's a pun.'

Savannah: 'What's a degustation?'

Guinea pig mother: 'It's like Hazel's breakfast. He enjoys a degustation of weetbix, human muesli and bran worms.'

The early pig catches the bran worm.

– Proverb

Framed

ALL NIGHT LONG a blonde guinea pig haunted Merridy's dreams. He was large, sleek and one-eyed. He hovered over the landscape like an enormous golden blimp, suspended by flimsy -looking angel wings. Those wings don't look strong enough to hold up an enormous golden blimp, Merridy dreamed vaguely, watching the apparition float about in a pleasantly blue sky. The blimp fixed her with his eye, and Merridy, struck painfully in the chest with a hefty remorse for dreaming the word 'blimp', immediately performed a penance under the blankets. Sixteen nocturnal genuflections plus promises of a magnificent feast of leftover Halloween pumpkin. Enough to feed at least sixteen guinea pigs. It eased the pain, at least to bearable levels, but Merridy groaned in her sleep as the enormous golden blimp flashed her with his halo. She tossed fretfully, muttering 'no more weetbix, no more weetbix'. She was having nightmares about overfeeding a vast golden guinea pig and giving him a heart attack. It was her mother's fault for feeding him breakfast-on-bed, weetbix and bran worms, day after day, instead of putting him out with the herd to burn off some fat. Then she, the guinea pig mother, couldn't stop him eating. In Merridy's dream the blonde guinea pig looked at her mother, the guinea pig grandmother, and her mother, the guinea pig grandmother, fed him another weetbix. My mother is hypnotised, thought Merridy.

On waking, on this auspicious first of November morning, Merridy had a colossal headache, as if something large had landed on it in the night. She couldn't think what was auspicious about the first of November. It wasn't her birthday. It wasn't the solstice. It definitely wasn't Christmas. Halloween was over and Guy Fawkes obsolete. Australians didn't do gunpowder, treason and plot, just copious quantities of pumpkin entrails.

Must feed the guinea pigs, she thought.

Then she remembered the flashing halo and sat bolt upright in bed.

'Holy cows and saddleback hogs!' she groaned, and squinted up at the Royal Portrait, from whence His Highness Hazel, the one-eyed Pig God, gazed down upon his mother. His good eye, his languid eye, his powerful and benevolent eye, observed her knowingly, and she felt its glance penetrate her heart centre, the space between her eyebrows, her left thumb, and what might feasibly be her liver.

It hurt like the devil.

What I need, Merridy thought in alarm, is someone to light a load of gunpowder under my bottom. That might shock my brain into thinking of a plot.

'What?' she squeaked. 'What plot?'

The halo flashed and Merridy was struck with a startling vision. It was of a hefty book with an imposing golden guinea pig on its glossy cover.

'But I'm an editor, not a novelist,' she said.

The halo flashed persistently in the corner of her left eye, which was now wide open.

'I edit *other* people's plots.' She breathed deeply, hoping to blot out the sense of impending doom.

'And guinea pigs is a theme, not a plot!' She closed her eyes, hoping to erase both portrait and lurking halo.

'I can't write an entire novel about guinea pigs!' she yelped.

And Merridy, mother to eleven guinea pigs past and present, said 'No!'

But the Pig God Hazel, like the Universe at large, does not do 'can't'.

Hazel the Pig God Rules.

Hazel Pink-Ears Little Nipper Pugh. Once Hazel tiny-weeny baby. Now deceased in a corporeal sense, but in every other, alive and wielding that eye to his better advantage. Mao Tse Hazel looks at Merridy from the bedhead, the dressing table, the kitchen bench, the bathroom mirror. His Lordship sits above her desk, exquisite in his blonde pelt, groomed to perfection, whiskers at attention, the rose-petal ear proclaiming his pedigree. He exited this earthly paradise too soon, of a heart attack feasibly linked to an overenthusiastic taste for weetbix, but reincarnated with angel wings and a persistent habit of loitering about Merridy's subconscious.

Hence the largest photograph in the bedroom is of Hazel One-Eye, organised via a useful minion after the burial ceremony of the said Hazel. The Royal Portrait had been a royal stroke of genius, for it kept Hazel's mother where he liked her. And the useful minion had been dispensed with, having outlived his usefulness. Unfortunately for Merridy, she had not outlived hers.

The Pig God Hazel eyed her speculatively from above the meditation shrine.

'Absolutely not!' she said emphatically. 'I refuse!'

Hazel One-Eye fixed his one eye balefully in her direction. Merridy felt somewhat impaled, but rebellious. With a pointed huff she rolled out of bed and staggered into the kitchen.

It was early morning. The sun shone, a promising but unreliable omen of things to come. Perhaps it would be a shorts day. Or perhaps it would snow forcefully halfway down the mountain and everyone would be caught with their shorts on.

Merridy looked out of the window. A sailboat drifted past the leading light far below on the River Derwent. The view was, as always, sensational. But Merridy's attention was diverted by the sight of a small guinea pig. He was ginger, with a ginger crown, and poised expectantly on an upturned cardboard box.

Merridy filled a glass with water from the tap. She drank it. The Halloween pumpkin grinned at her from the table. It was an evil grin, with shades of gloating in it. For heaven's sake, she thought. She peeled a banana quickly and tossed the peels into a row of boxes. There was a rustle of excitement, and Jupiter jumped hastily off his throne to claim his breakfast.

Then she stepped wearily into the bathroom, where Hazel eyed her from the basin mirror. She sat on the toilet. Hazel watched from behind the toilet door. She closed her eyes. Hazel flashed his halo inside her forehead. She flushed the loo. The halo flashed in unison.

Merridy turned on the shower, wanting to flush the halo down the plughole. She stood under the steamy blast, trying to clear her head of residual aches. But as the water heated her skin, pounding on her head and shoulders, a pinkish glimmer replaced the agitated halo. It was a glimmer of hope.

Hazel shifted comfortably on his perch above the basin.

'There is an extensive guinea pig subculture,' mused Merridy as the water began to ease her headache, 'who will flock to read a book about guinea pigs.' Her skin glowed pink under the heated water and her heart swelled as she contemplated the vast underworld of guinea pig fanatics and cavy slaves, all waiting to read such literature.

Hazel watched with approval. His mother was finally on the right track.

'And I may become rich and famous. Ouch!' She felt a poke under the ribcage. Hazel didn't care if his mother became a universal laughing stock so long as He, The Royal Boar, became rich and famous. 'Perhaps it will win a substantial literary prize,' she continued, 'for being the first-ever guinea pig novel!' Merridy was jumping the gun, since the first-ever guinea pig novel had yet to be written, but her brain was on a fast-track to success. 'And then I will be able to fund Pig Heaven, my guinea pig orphanage, and eventually, a global network of guinea pig orphanages!' The halo flashed a strobe of applause.

And so Hazel begat the first-ever guinea pig novel, *Pig Tails*.

Part One

The Angel Hazel

1

Caveat emptor

ONCE UPON A LONG TIME AGO one year in April, with the sweet grass scented heavily by warm sunshine, Merridy went to the Hobart Guinea Pig Show.

The Hobart Guinea Pig Show was underway in a subterranean lair at the Royal Hobart Showgrounds. It had the appearance of an event known only to an inner circle of dedicated guinea pig breeders and rather fierce guinea pig groomers. Merridy felt like an intruder. She felt nervous and conspicuous.

The competitors had on display their fattest and finest guinea pigs. The guinea pigs were displayed in rows. Each guinea pig was groomed to a gloss, placed on a small carpet, and flattened by hand into a guinea pancake. It was a strange sight, the sight of rows of flat glossy guinea pancakes sitting on little carpets.

Merridy soon forgot she was an intruder. She waited for the guinea pigs to take off on their tiny flying carpets. There were blonde pigs, black pigs, Friesian-cow-type pigs, whorled and curled pigs, albino pigs, and a guinea pig like an English sheepdog. The English sheepdog pig had hair down to the ground and beyond. It was hard to tell which was the front end. Perhaps the English sheepdog pig didn't know either.

A stern guinea pig judge began walking down the lines of pigs. She poked and prodded and did things with their hair. She flipped their rose-petal ears inside and out. The guinea pigs sat there like miniature sphinxes with blank expressions. Merridy wondered if they were on drugs. Surely it was unnatural for a guinea pig to sit like an Egyptian stone statue while a large human poked its orifices. Were they fed valium with their carrots?

The guinea pig judge finally stopped poking about and produced rosettes. Royal blue, crimson, bright gold, and emerald. The English sheepdog pig was presented with a royal blue number. It looked splendid with his hairstyle but his owner whipped it away and pinned it on his own lapel. The sheepdog pig remained unmoved. Perhaps, thought Merridy, it's had an overdose and has subsided into a coma?

Along the wall opposite the flying carpets stood a series of long tables with small compartments on top. Merridy went to inspect. The compartments were filled with fragrant yellow hay. Small bulges wriggled and squirmed beneath it. Oh my soul! thought Merridy. Guinea pig babies!

Merridy's inner bank teller went onto red alert. Remember, said the inner bank teller, you came to look, not buy!

Merridy ignored her inner bank teller and began a thorough examination of the guinea pig babies. There were tiny white guinea pig babies with pink eyes. There were grey ones with white blotches. A very messy guinea pig baby had three kinds of hair – grey, black, and yellow – with whorls shooting in every direction. He looked extremely confused but unbelievably cute.

Merridy's inner bank teller went into emergency mode. Look, don't buy! Look, don't buy!

But Merridy was, to all intents and purposes, absolutely deaf.

A tiny blonde guinea pig lay splayed on top of a box of hay. The blonde tresses matched the golden bedding. Delicate pink feet sat daintily under the tiny round torso. The rose petal ears were petite and perfect. The black eyes were shiny and half-closed.

Merridy was having a heart attack. Well, a love attack, which is more or less the same thing. The tiny blonde piglet was by far the smallest in the visible herd, and the only one lying right on top of the hay, out in the open for all to see. The tiny blonde piglet looked like a movie star. Quite undisturbed by the crowds of onlookers, the tiny blonde pig seemed used to adulation.

For Merridy it was instantaneous. She didn't care if it cost an arm, a leg, and her lifetime supply of chocolate. She had to have this guinea pig.

When she could speak, Merridy approached the guinea pig breeder behind the long tables.

'He is a boy,' the guinea pig breeder said firmly. Merridy, who was inexperienced in the matter of guinea pigs, took her word for it. 'And he's a pedigree,' said the guinea pig breeder proudly. 'A purebred.' The breeder lifted the tiny blonde beast into the air. 'A pedigree cream boar,' she said, pointing at the creature's adorably tiny rump.

Merridy was impressed. A pedigree cream boar. The breeder obviously knew her stuff.

The pedigree cream boar looked coolly at the breeder and at Merridy from his undignified position in the air. They were too focused on their transaction to notice.

'He has papers,' said the guinea pig breeder. 'I will give you his family tree for your records.'

Merridy's eyes widened.

'That'll be twenty dollars,' said the breeder, holding out her free hand for the cash.

Merridy's heart thumped. The little angel-pig was hers. He was a pedigree cream boar. For a princely sum of twenty Australian dollars. Hers. To have and to hold. For better for worse. In sickness and health. Till death do us part! She did an excited inner dance, so that the guinea pig breeder wouldn't think she was a lunatic.

The guinea pig breeder put the tiny blonde boar into a cardboard box.

But, Merridy thought, I cannot have a lone pig. It would be cruel to have a lonely baby boar, all by himself when I am not at home.

She looked at the tiny angel boar. 'Who would you like as a friend?' she asked.

The angel boar just stared at Merridy.

She went hunting among the other compartments. It was difficult to see any whole piglets because they were burrowing and snoozing under the hay. Then she spotted a batch of plump brown triplets. One of them had a white rosette on his forehead. Very handsome with that hairdo, thought Merridy.

Merridy went to consult the guinea pig breeder. She wanted another boy pig and needed someone to check. It was important to have two boy pigs to avoid ending up with hundreds of guinea pig babies eating her out of house and home. Two boy pigs would be perfect.

'Yes,' said the guinea pig breeder. 'The brown pig with the rosette is a boy. But he is not a pedigree.' Merridy didn't mind. All she wanted was a companion for her blonde angel and this little fellow looked docile and friendly and he would do. 'You'll do, pig, you'll do,' she said ecstatically under her breath as the guinea pig breeder pocketed another five Australian dollars and popped the brown piglet into the box with the blonde angel.

What a marvellous pair, Merridy thought, her heart walloping wildly as she carried her precious cargo to a small white vehicle with fishes all over it. This was her transport, the fishmobile. 'Although today,' she said to her cargo, 'it's a pigmobile.'

She placed the cardboard box onto the floor in front of the passenger seat. Then she could drive and watch the piglets at the same time. Well, not exactly at the same time but out of the corner of her eye to avoid accidents.

On the way home, her brain churned busily. 'It's a big decision choosing baby names. Even for guinea pig babies,' she said.

'Caramel and Honey?' She glanced down at her tiny charges. The brown piglet was half on top of the blonde angel.

'Almond and Peanut?' The brown piglet's little black eyes were popping.

'Peaches and Cream?' The blonde angel's eyes were closed.

'Too much on the food theme,' Merridy ruminated as she coasted down the Brooker Highway, taking care to drive steadily for the comfort of her passengers.

Then she remembered a favourite childhood novel, *Watership Down*. It was all about rabbits. There were rabbits named after flora, like Dandelion and Speedwell. And there was a hero rabbit, the valiant boy-rabbit, Hazel. 'Ah!' said Merridy, 'A name that reminds me of hazelnuts – yum! – and hazel thickets with lush green leaves in an English countryside.' She imagined the angel Hazel posed in the middle of all that verdant green. 'It would set off your blonde fur beautifully,' she said to the dozing angel. 'Yes, Hazel, that's you!'

'And,' she said to the little brown piglet, whose head was now wedged under Hazel's bottom as if his life depended on it, 'you are more reddish-brown than chocolate-brown. Burnt Sienna?

No – too arty. Chai Latté? No,' she said, 'it just will not do to name you as if you're part of my restaurant reviews.'

Merridy pondered. His colouring reminded her of a chestnut style of horse. And like chestnuts when they are polished up and shiny. 'Chestnut,' she said. It had a wholesome, round, shiny ring to it. It brought to mind hot roasted chestnuts, chestnut trees in bloom, and well-groomed shiny stallions. 'Chestnut,' she said to the wedged brown piglet, 'Chestnut. Yes, that's you!'

Merridy turned up the driveway of her Green Street home and parked round the back. The tiny guinea pigs looked up at her from the floor of the fishmobile. 'Welcome home!' she announced. 'Welcome to Green Street, Hazel and Chestnut! Chestnut and Hazel! My baby guinea pigs!'

Chestnut looked anxious, and Hazel looked bored. He was waiting to be released onto that lovely green sward in Merridy's imagination.

2

What to feed a guinea pig

WHAT TO FEED BABY GUINEA PIGS? This was the question uppermost in Merridy's mind. New guinea pig mother, excited guinea pig mother, tentative guinea pig mother.

The sun shone down on the mountain and the sparkling blue River Derwent and into the Green Street garden. It was a beautiful day. A summery day. The rose bush arched across the falling-down shed in a cascade of fragrant pink blooms. It was a perfect day, with the mountain serene and well behaved, even though it was officially autumn. Hobartian seasons were unpredictable, but the guinea pig mother was in luck. It was the perfect day for feeding baby guinea pigs fresh green growing things from their new garden.

'Boys!' said Merridy. 'Welcome to Green Street!'

Then she stopped. Hazel watched her from the cardboard box. He was quite still, with a funny expression in his beautiful black eyes. Merridy felt uncomfortable. She couldn't be sure, but she had the distinct feeling that he was looking at her with a how-can-you-be-so-stupid look. This was a trifle unnerving, coming from a small blonde angel-pig.

Chestnut, on the other hand, looked alarmed. He peered furtively from behind Hazel's tiny torso, with a she-moves-I'm-gonna-run-for-it sort of look. Poor Chestnut. He was one-and-a-half times the size of the blonde angel, and hiding behind Hazel didn't work.

Merridy decided a meal of juicy grass would do the trick. It would distract Chestnut from the humanoid monster he obviously thought she was. It would please Hazel, whom she felt an inordinate need to please.

'Grass, boys!' she announced, feeling happy at the thought of this healthy offering. 'Grass!'

She lifted the cardboard box from the floor of the fishmobile. She set it gently on the lush Green Street lawn. 'Hazel and Chestnut!' she said. 'Chestnut and Hazel! My baby pigs!'

Merridy sat cross-legged on the grass, folding her long hippy skirt into a smooth hollow in her lap. This would be a good cradle-cum-playpen until further notice. It would prevent sudden dashes for freedom. An unpleasant image flashed into Merridy's mind. She winced. She saw herself chasing Hazel and Chestnut round and round the Green Street garden, tripping repeatedly over her long hippy skirt while the piglets escaped into holes beneath the falling-down house. Then, she knew, she would never find them. She would have to put 'Lost!' signs up and down Green Street. Battalions of neighbours would hunt for her guinea pigs and poke about the vegetation with sticks and it would all be futile because Hazel and Chestnut would have fallen into a nasty under-house abyss and be stuck. She would be known as the Irresponsible Guinea Pig Mother. Hazel and Chestnut would starve to death.

Merridy quickly put such thoughts aside before she broke into a cold sweat. Holy cannelloni! It was a big thing, being a guinea pig mother.

Merridy lifted tiny Hazel out of the cardboard box. He was soft and silky and very light. His pink ears caught the sunshine like the finest stained glass. She placed him carefully into the skirt-cradle, where he sat very still.

Then she lifted Chestnut out of the cardboard box, where he was hiding in a corner. 'Come on, little Chestnut,' she whispered. 'It's quite safe!' Chestnut felt silky too, and a bit heavier than Hazel. His eyes were bulging with fright. Merridy laid him carefully next to Hazel.

Then she leaned over and picked a handful of juicy grass.

'Here you are, boys!' she said. 'Beautiful juicy grass!'

An hour later Merridy was a little desperate.

Hazel looked bored. Chestnut had burrowed underneath Hazel. It was a silly sight, Chestnut's head buried under Hazel's tummy, and his fine round bottom sticking up. But Merridy did not laugh, for her baby pigs would not eat. They would not eat the beautiful juicy grass. They would not eat the bright yellow dandelions. They would not eat the white lawn daisies. They would not eat scarlet pimpernel, or rose petals, or forget-me-nots.

Merridy had run out of weeds. Her legs were numb. It was very hot in the sun. She needed an umbrella, and a guinea pig dietitian.

'Oats!' she said. 'Maybe guinea pigs like oats!'

Tenderly she lifted Hazel off Chestnut's head and placed him back into the cardboard box. She lifted the exhumed Chestnut off her long hippy skirt and placed him next to Hazel. Chestnut cowered behind Hazel's insignificant bottom.

Merridy stood up on a severe case of pins and needles. When she could reliably direct her feet, she carried the cardboard box carefully up the fire escape into her Green Street eyrie.

'Welcome to my eyrie!' she said to her precious charges. 'Welcome to Flat Three!' She looked around her cheerful kitchen, with its primrose-yellow and lavender-blue paintwork and large wide window with coloured glass bottles along the sill. 'I will have an excellent view,' said Merridy to Hazel and Chestnut, 'of your playpen on the lawn – when we have one.' It was true. Her eyrie looked one way to the mountain and one way to the sea, and in the middle, the kitchen window looked out upon the Green Street garden. It was the perfect spot for a guinea pig playpen, and the window was the perfect viewpoint for a guinea pig mother.

Chestnut scrabbled frantically, trying to bury himself further beneath Hazel, and Hazel looked tolerant, if slightly irked. Merridy gently placed the box on the hideously striped kitchen carpet, and turned it carefully onto one side, in case any piglet would like to explore. She tipped Hazel and Chestnut very delicately toward the carpet.

Then she set about the kitchen. She found rolled oats. She found pink lady apples. She found a crooked but crunchy carrot. She found a shallow dish and filled it with fresh water. She laid the guinea pig feast before Chestnut and Hazel. 'Boys!' she said. 'Hazel and Chestnut! Eat up!'

Hazel was splayed out on the striped carpet like an undercooked golden pancake. Chestnut was hunched into a ball, like an oversized gulab jamun. Merridy was ravenous, and could have eaten several pancakes and gulab jamun with rose-petal and maple syrup, chopped pink lady apple on the side and a mammoth dollop of vanilla bean ice cream, but since these were not available, she sat on her blue sparkly couch and ate a carrot.

Chestnut and Hazel ignored the guinea pig feast.

'Oh dear!' said Merridy. 'What's a guinea pig mother to do?'

The undercooked pancake and the gulab jamun remained motionless.

'Aha!' she said.

Merridy sat down at her Apple laptop. She googled 'guinea pig fodder'. Google helpfully and comprehensively offered two hundred thousand five hundred and sixty-three relevant links. Merridy picked the first. She read:

Feed your guinea pigs daily greens, copious fresh hay, and guinea pig pellets or muesli. Guinea pigs, like humans, cannot make Vitamin C inside the body and must eat Vitamin C-rich fruits and vegetables regularly.

There followed a helpful and comprehensive list of guinea-pig friendly foods:

fresh juicy grass
bright yellow dandelions
clover
white lawn daisies
rose petals

Merridy stopped. Perhaps she had defective guinea pigs. Surely not! Or maybe baby guinea pigs drank milk out of a bottle?

She googled 'guinea pig baby fodder'.

Google offered a mind-boggling number of guinea pig baby fodder authorities. Merridy picked the first. It said:

Guinea pigs are born fully formed and furred. They can eat hay and dry food straight away, and will suckle from their mother for up to six weeks.

Merridy remembered the guinea pig breeder saying that Hazel was newly weaned, at six weeks old. And Chestnut was a whole three months grown. That's why he was one-and-a-half times the size of the blonde angel. 'What is dry food?' she wondered.

Merridy returned to the comprehensive and helpful list of guinea-pig friendly foods.

capsicum
tomato
oats
beetroot
brussels sprouts

'Brussels sprouts!' exclaimed Merridy, impressed. She detested brussels sprouts despite their endearing stature. If guinea pigs ate brussels sprouts, they had gumption. She read on:

cabbage
carrot
pumpkin
banana
baby spinach

It sounded like a very healthy diet. 'I will incorporate aspects of guinea-pig friendly fodder into my own meal routine,' said Merridy decisively. 'But no brussels sprouts!'

Then she read:

Guinea pigs do not eat potatoes, onion or garlic.
Feeding iceberg lettuce is dangerous and causes diarrhoea.

Merridy didn't like the idea of giving her babies the runs. She would ban iceberg lettuce from Flat Three and use baby spinach in her salads.

Sighing, Merridy put down her Apple laptop and picked up a pink lady to crunch on.

She glanced down at the motionless piglets. Hazel was still in undercooked pancake mode and Chestnut was still poorly disguised as an oversized gulab jamun. Perhaps the striped carpet was making them queasy. It did that when you weren't used to it.

Merridy found an old newspaper for the guinea pig babies' new bed. She found a pink sparkly plastic box, and lined it with the old newspaper. Hazel watched. Merridy felt uncomfortable. She couldn't be sure, but Hazel seemed to be watching with a disapproving air. Perhaps he doesn't like pink, thought Merridy. 'But it will look very pretty with your fur,' she said.

She tore up strips of newspaper to make comfy bedding for her boys. She put in a small dish of oats, pink lady and carrot. She put in the shallow dish of fresh water. She picked the guinea pigs up, one at a time, and put them into the comfy newspaper bed. Hazel stared, and Chestnut buried himself under the newspaper.

Then a miracle happened.

Hazel started eating.

Merridy was ecstatic. She now felt like a fifty-percent-successful guinea pig mother, which was a great improvement, even if Hazel's chosen fodder was not strictly nutritious. It was better than eating nothing at all. It was progress.

Merridy carried the pink sparkly box into the bedroom. She placed it next to her queen-sized pink bed, which glowed in the afternoon sun streaming through the window. The mountain had a cloud on top, but it was still a beautiful day. She lay down, hoisting Chestnut onto her tummy and stroking his chestnut fur. 'You will get used to your humanoid monster mother,' she said. 'You will become a relaxed, laid-back, restful pig, with a fine bottom to boot.' She pulled the edge of her hippy top over Chestnut, to help him feel safe, and cradled him beneath her palms. She did not know that one day Chestnut would become a laid-back very expensive pig whose veterinary adventures would get her into a lot of trouble.

The dainty angel looked up from his meal, his pink lips demurely visible and his beautiful black eyes as innocent as a newborn Bambi's. He looked pure, virginal and exquisite.

'It has been a big day,' said Merridy to her baby boars. 'It has been an auspicious day,' she said, which was an understatement of cosmic proportions, but fortunately for Merridy's peace of mind, she had no idea.

'And now it's time for a siesta,' announced Merridy, not noticing the virginal angel's air of smug complacency. She closed her eyes.

Merridy and Chestnut were lulled to sleep by the soporific sounds of Hazel chewing his newspaper.

3

This earthly paradise

MERRIDY SLUMBERED BLISSFULLY on her pink bed in the sunshine. She dreamt a giant guinea pig was tearing enormous slabs of peanut brittle into tiny pieces for her exclusive and pleasurable consumption. Chestnut, snuggled on his mother's comfy tummy under her warm hands, dreamt he was in a pink cocoon with a humanoid monster trying unsuccessfully to break into it with a pair of pliers. His ears twitched. Hazel shredded newspaper loudly in the pink sparkly box.

Two hundred and seven kilometres from this harmonious scene, a small boy leapt up and down on a trampoline. Up, up, into the sun, down, down, onto the trampoline. He somersaulted impressively, bounced three times in a seated position and flipped onto his stomach.

Alexander Scott was seven years old. He was Merridy's nephew.

Alexander Scott would become a champion trampolinist in slinky white trousers and a shiny singlet. Meanwhile, he practised leaps and bounds with concentrated enthusiasm, sporting a rainbow tie-dye T-shirt from his hippy aunty.

Alexander Scott lived two hundred and seven kilometres north and slightly west of Green Street. His garden sat beneath a tall brick two-storey house. The garden was studded with rose trees which flaunted gloriously scented pink and red roses. They also brandished an assortment of deadly thorns. Alexander Scott's mother had placed the trampoline as far from the rose trees as possible, to avoid accidental impalements.

On a patch of luscious lawn sat a large chicken coop. The chicken coop was covered in chickenwire. It looked like a chicken coop for bantams because it was very low. A normal-sized chicken would get a crook neck. It would be a crook-necked chook.

Alexander Scott waved cheerfully at the chicken coop from his position on the trampoline. It was an excellent position, being high off the ground, and afforded a bird's eye view into the chicken coop. It looked quiet and empty. Perhaps the chooks were resting indoors to avoid crooking their chook-necks.

'Alexaaaaaander!'

A loud maternal summons from the upper storey of the brick house caused Alexander Scott to catapult off his trampoline and make his way up to the kitchen door. Alexander's mother passed him a large bucket. In the bucket were food scraps. Pumpkin peels, apple cores, carrot tops, and a large broccoli stump. This was an earth-friendly household which recycled compostable matter.

'Thanks, Mum!' said Alexander Scott cheerfully.

He carried the bucket of compostable matter down to the garden. He hefted the lid off the chicken coop. Still not a chicken to be seen. Not a rooster, not a bantam, not even an egg.

Alexander emptied the compostables onto the ground in

the chicken coop. 'Wheek wheek wheek!' he called, in a funny squeaky voice. It seemed a strange voice for calling chickens. 'Wheek wheek wheek!'

But out of the roosting box doorway poked a nose. It definitely wasn't a chicken nose. It wasn't beaky enough. It wasn't even a beak. It was pointy, but in a soft, rodent sort of way. It was furry, with beautiful orange fur. The nostrils were brown and sniffing.

Behind the furry orange pointy nose with brown sniffing nostrils, Alexander Scott could see two shiny dark eyes. Suddenly the furry orange snout shot out of the roosting box doorway, followed by a roundish animal on short legs. The animal had fur all over and a furry crest running along its back, like a Ridgeback dog. On its forehead was a tiny white spot.

Before Alexander Scott could squeak another 'wheek', the animal was followed by a second furball on stumpy limbs. This one was the shade of a delicious bar of dark chocolate, with a white stripe along its nose and a rosette on its forehead.

'Wheek wheek wheek!' they answered, scurrying to and fro across the chicken coop and falling upon the compostables with gusto. 'Wheek wheek wheek!'

Alexander Scott laughed at the excited furballs and picked one up. 'Hello Choklit!' he crooned, cuddling his catch while it squeaked and wheeked in apparent delight. 'Would you like some grass?' Alexander picked a grass blade and fed it into Choklit's mouth. Choklit ate it like spaghetti. The grass blade disappeared quickly, as if it was being sucked up by a miniature vacuum cleaner. Choklit sucked up another grass blade, a dandelion stalk, and a white lawn daisy. Then Alexander put him back with the compostables. Choklit sucked up a pumpkin peel.

Alexander reached for the orange furball. The orange furball disappeared speedily under the roosting box. Alexander tipped the roosting box up to get a grip on the escapee. The furball screamed in protest, but once in Alexander's arms, shrieked hoarsely in furry bliss. Alexander tickled the furry tummy, and the furry chin, and stroked the little white spot. 'Hello Little Spot!' he said.

Two hundred and seven kilometres south and slightly east, Hazel shredded newspaper with vigour while Chestnut and Merridy dreamed. The sun sparkled off the great Derwent estuary, and the sky was clear, and seagulls called their plaintive calls into the sea air. The mountain's shadow crept across the hills towards Green Street, where the guinea pig mother and Chestnut slept, and the long autumn twilight cast its aura over the city. Small boats bobbed on the waters, their sails translucent in the setting sun, and a pod of dolphins frolicked out in the bay. A cockatoo swooped over the Green Street house, cawing raucously, and settled to eating the fruits of a nearby walnut tree. On a warm still night, Hobart was the most beautiful place on earth.

Alexander Scott hefted the lid back onto the chicken coop and took the empty bucket to his mother. 'Don't forget to clean the chicken coop,' she reminded him. Alexander sighed. He loved his guinea pigs dearly, but they made so much mess. They were now one year old, and as they grew, so did their poos. And it was more risky holding them on his lap, since their bladders had also expanded, and while this meant they could hold on for longer, when they couldn't, it was a lot wetter.

Alexander Scott took down some old newspaper for bedding, and wandered back to the chicken coop. Choklit and Little Spot were still sucking up pumpkin peels. Alexander hopped on the trampoline and performed an athletic somersault. Guinea pig father, and tramp-champ to be. The sun shone hotly on the rose trees and lifted the scent into the sultry air.

4

How it all began

IN LATER ERAS, even with hindsight, it was hard to say whose fault it was.

Was it Alexander Scott's, with his plaintive pleas for a pet? Or was it his mother's, who said yes? Perhaps it was Choklit's, with his irresistible good nature, or Little Spot's, with his authoritative ridge? Or was it simply an overwhelming planetary alignment with unusual consequences?

It was difficult to pin the blame on a diminutive angel-pig who was not yet born at that point on the timeline of earthly history. And nobody imagined a furry and pugnacious prime mover setting things in train from a parallel dimension.

And so the cause remained mysterious.

But the timing was clear.

It began in the year then called 2005 by human inhabitants of the island of Tasmania and around the Australian continent and in the western world generally. To be precise, it was called

2005 AD, which means, two thousand and five years Ano Domini, which means (in Latin), after the birth of a certain important deity, although some called it 2005 CE, which means (in English) of the Common Era, because they preferred other deities, or none at all.

And in 2005 AD the important deity Hazel had not been born yet, but that was when it all began. Because in the year 2005 AD, in late summer, the first guinea pigs arrived in Alexander Scott's household. About this there is no doubt.

Choklit and Little Spot were the Originals. They were chosen and named by Alexander Scott. And they became the Catalysts, because they caused Merridy, the guinea pig mother, to go to the Hobart Guinea Pig Show. And that changed Merridy's life and the course of guinea pig history forever.

And thus began the Guinea Pig Era.

And when it all began, in the year later known as Year One of the Guinea Pig Era, Merridy was far away at the very Top End of Australia. She was four thousand four hundred kilometres north of her Green Street eyrie, sampling a variety of tropical menus for research purposes, and writing a swatch of restaurant reviews. In between she swam in turquoise pools under the palm trees, and sent regular and enviable postcards to those left behind in the unreliable Tasmanian climate.

And she received an unexpected phone call.

It was evening, and Merridy was returned to her place of repose. Merridy's kind host answered the cordless telephone and brought it over to where she reclined floppily on a soft tropical sofa. As she listened to the phone call, she sat bolt upright and made astonishing squealing sounds and gurgles. Merridy's kind host brought across a glass of water in case she was choking.

At the other end of the line, Alexander Scott made an announcement. 'Gurgle, splutter, squeak!' gargled Merridy.

'They are babies,' said Alexander to his gargling aunty. 'They are brothers. They come from the same mother. I chose the best two. They are boys.'

'Honk, huff, puff!' coughed Merridy.

'I have named them Choklit and Little Spot!' said Alexander proudly.

Merridy did not say anything at all. She felt as if an arrow had lodged in her breastbone, the sort that happens at the onset of a fatal attraction. Painful, heady, and irresistible.

'I was going to call them Choklit and Fudge,' said Alexander Scott, who emulated his aunty when it came to food, 'but I chose Little Spot because he has a tiny white spot on his forehead. He is a Ridgeback guinea pig. And Choklit is a Crested guinea pig!'

When Merridy could speak, she congratulated her nephew on his supreme choice of pets. 'I can't wait to see them!' she squeaked, while her kind host wondered if someone had announced the birth of quintuplets.

Alexander Scott felt a sense of triumph as he ended the phone call. *That* had impressed his aunty. Ha! He was the proud owner of two guinea pigs. He was a guinea pig father!

Merridy lay back on the soft tropical sofa feeling spaced out from excitement. Her kind host went to barbecue the sausages, wondering who had given birth.

And one year later came the Young Ones: the timid but shapely Chestnut, and the exquisitely well-bred Hazel. And the Guinea Pig Era began to gather momentum.

That evening, after Merridy and Chestnut had woken and Merridy had offered her baby boars slivers of pumpkin, which Hazel had eaten and Chestnut, judging from his expression, rejected as the work of the devil, Merridy made two important phone calls.

The first was a phone call to Alexander Scott. Alexander uttered suitable guffaws and squawks and scampered off shouting to his mother, leaving the telephone hanging for a whole five minutes. Merridy didn't mind, as she was occupied with the Angel Hazel on her lap, trying to cosset from him a sound. The Angel Hazel was looking obstinate, which in a delicate and very small creature seemed incongruous, and he was silent.

When Alexander Scott returned, he asked several expert questions, such as, 'Have you checked for their testicles?' and dispensed expert advice, such as, 'Make sure you have a towel on your lap in case they wee.' It was useful having an expert guinea pig father as a nephew, and Merridy fetched a towel at once, in case of getting wet.

The second phone call was to the ancestral household. The ancestral household was near Alexander Scott's, high up on a hillside looking across the beautiful Tamar Valley.

'You have two more grandpigs – Hazel and Chestnut!' Merridy announced proudly to her mother, who rushed off to interrupt Old and Young Grandpa's tv viewing before she could say, 'Hazel is a pedigree cream boar.' Her mother returned and said excitedly, 'Like Hazel in *Watership Down*!' She was both well read and quick off the mark, and Merridy said, 'Yes, Hazel is named after a literary hero!' And then she told her mother about the Hobart Guinea Pig Show, and the rows of flying carpets and the fierce guinea pig groomers. 'Hazel is a pedigree cream boar. He has papers and a family tree,' she said, 'and cost twenty dollars. And Chestnut is a handsome mongrel with a rosette, and cost only five dollars.'

'Flying carpets!' exclaimed her mother, and 'Pedigree cream boar!' and 'Only five dollars!' She was a responsive conversationalist and very enthusiastic about guinea pigs. 'I want to go to a guinea pig show!'

'Hazel,' said Merridy, 'seems a confident pig despite his diminutive stature. And Chestnut is an anxious pig with a fine bottom.'

'Gosh!' said the guinea pig grandmother excitedly, and 'Can I speak to Hazel and Chestnut?'

But the diminutive furry angel was still silent, so Merridy put him back in his pink sparkly box with the handsome but anxious mongrel, who dived underneath the angel's tiny tummy with relief. 'Chestnut is too anxious to speak on the telephone,' said Merridy to her mother, 'and I'm afraid Hazel won't.'

That night the moon shone down on Merridy as she dreamed in her pink bed. Her new companions slumbered by her side in their pink sparkly box. Chestnut slumbered restlessly with his head under Hazel's delicate golden flank, and Hazel slumbered comfortably on the cushion that was Chestnut's head.

Two hundred and seven kilometres further north on the heart-shaped island that is Tasmania, a small boy dreamed about baby guinea pigs on a trampoline. His mother looked in on her sleeping son on her way to bed, and in the chicken coop in the garden, Choklit and Little Spot snuggled like peas in a pod.

A little further down the Tamar Valley, the ancestral household was quiet in the moonlight. Old Grandpa got up to check that it wasn't time for his shower, which it wasn't, and Young Grandpa went to the toilet. The guinea pig grandmother was fast asleep.

Merridy stirred in her sleep, for she was dreaming of being a little girl in Africa, walking along the road to school with two guinea pigs in tow. The guinea pigs were well disciplined and docile, and followed her like miniature dogs. In her classroom the children crowded around, and she felt inordinately proud, and placed the guinea pigs on the teacher's desk on a tiny crimson flying carpet. The guinea pigs, a small blonde one and a larger brown one, sat as still as two furry statues, and one of them, the small blonde one, delivered a small token onto the teacher's clean writing pad. The guinea pigs were an unqualified success.

5

A matter of baubles

MANY WERE THE DESCRIPTORS thrown the guinea pig mother's way in the first week. They lacked imagination but were flattering in the extreme, so Merridy resisted the urge of her inner thesaurus to offer alternatives to ardent but repetitive utterances of 'sooo cu-ute!' 'sooo swee-eet!' and 'sooo adooorable!' She ignored guests who suggested that the exquisite Angel Hazel and the handsome Cherub Chestnut might bite.

Chestnut had turned out a great eater, and possibly a great comfort-eater, as once he found his eating function, he did not stop. He ate pink lady and oats and pumpkin. He ate cucumber and fresh grass and white lawn daisies and broccoli stumps. He gobbled carrots as if his life depended on it, and slurped up banana peels as if a famine were imminent.

Hazel, to his mother's approval, had expanded his culinary taste well beyond the *Mercury*. 'Newspaper,' said Merridy to the blonde angel, 'has plenty of fibre but minimal nutrition, and definitely no Vitamin C.' The blonde angel nibbled a newspaper shred carelessly. 'And you can't make your own Vitamin C, so you must eat fresh vegetables daily.' The blonde angel stared at his mother, and if he had not been a small guinea pig, his mother might have thought it was a resentful stare. But the guinea pig mother dismissed such thoughts, because the Angel Hazel was pure and unsullied, and a very small guinea pig indeed.

Since her pivotal excursion to the Hobart Guinea Pig Show, Merridy had entertained numerous inquisitive spectators and hamster-enthusiasts at her Green Street eyrie. The uninformed latter contingent could now tell the difference between a common hamster and a much-superior guinea pig. It was a little tiresome repeating the words 'guinea pig' every time a well-meaning but ignorant visitor said 'hamster', but Merridy was grateful for her visitors and exercised her patience.

It was surprising how the arrival of two small rodents could generate such fervour. 'I am amazed,' said Merridy to her mother, the guinea pig grandmother, on the telephone, 'that so many people like guinea pigs. Even if they think they are hamsters,' she added.

'Maybe it's their build,' she speculated. 'Their round cuddly bodies, with twiddly little legs.'

'Lips!' said the guinea pig grandmother. 'It's their little lips!' It was true that guinea pigs had the cutest mouths in the known universe. Their top lips were cleft into two delicate curves, and the pout of the lower lip was utterly endearing. Chestnut and Hazel had perfect pink lips.

'And their squeaks!' said Merridy, who had now successfully squeaked both Hazel and Chestnut. The Angel Hazel, as might be expected, had a clear musical squeak, and the Mongrel Chestnut, once he had been warmed up, had a squeaky door squeak. There is nothing so pleasurable as two squeaky guinea pigs in one's lap, thought Merridy warmly, even if one of them needs oiling.

'Yes,' said the guinea pig grandmother. 'They are so affectionate, and the best thing about them is their squeaks!' One could have argued that the best thing about a pedigree cream boar was his breeding, but the Angel Hazel was equally blessed with exquisite looks and enchanting squeaks. Chestnut on the other hand was blessed with an abundance of rump, which showed signs of increasing after a whole week's non-stop eating. It was hard not to want to squeeze such an abundant rump.

Today the guinea pigs were to be viewed by an important visitor, and Merridy was full of anticipation. 'You have an important visitor coming,' she said to her baby boars. 'He is an artist and a psychologist.' It was true. Hector Protector had an eye for beauty, and was a person of intellect with a triple degree. 'He is my best friend,' said Merridy. Hazel looked at his mother with an inscrutable expression, but she did not notice. 'And he is an excellent advisor,' said Merridy, thinking that she might need advising on matters like the psychology of comfort eating.

Hector Protector arrived in due course. 'This,' said Merridy to Hazel and Chestnut, 'is Hector Protector.' Hazel and Chestnut were in their pink sparkly box for the occasion. 'Actually,' she explained, 'his real name is something posher, for use when he is being a psychologist. But I call him Hector Protector. And so can you.'

'Hazel is a pedigree cream boar,' she said proudly to Hector Protector. 'With papers and a family tree. He is seven weeks old. He is named after the hero-rabbit in *Watership Down*.' Hector Protector chuckled and tickled Hazel on the top of his head. Merridy was pleased that he didn't say, '*Watership Down*?' with a question mark, as if she was referring to an obscure text in a foreign language. 'What a beautiful creature,' said Hector

Protector. 'He looks like a little angel!' 'Yes,' said Merridy, 'he is the Angel Hazel.' The Angel Hazel stared up at his large bearded visitor.

'And Chestnut,' said Merridy, 'is a mongrel boar, and he is three months and one week old, and a nervous pig.' Perhaps, she thought, Hector Protector could advise on what to do in cases of nerves. Hector Protector smiled at the sight of the little brown piglet with his white rosette, and reached to tickle his forehead. Chestnut's eyes popped and he dived under the shredded newspaper with the speed of a rocket. 'Goodness me!' said Hector Protector. 'He is a very nervous pig!'

Hector Protector inspected the Angel Hazel further, while Merridy put on the kettle for brewing hot chocolate. 'He looks intelligent,' said Hector Protector, and was rewarded with a did-you-really-think-I-was-stupid look. 'And feisty,' said Hector Protector.

And then came the question, which had been asked by too many previous visitors and was making Merridy nervous.

'How can you tell that Hazel is a boar?'

And this was the crux of the matter.

Although, to be accurate, there was no crux.

Chestnut and Hazel, the guinea pig breeder had assured Merridy, were boys. This was essential to avoid multiplication, at which guinea pigs were expert. And exponential population growth in Flat Three would have delightful but inconvenient consequences, such as being eaten out of house and home by hundreds of guinea pig babies. It would be irresponsible to allow such consequences, and so Merridy had chosen the mongrel boy Chestnut as companion to her pedigree cream boar.

When the seventh well-meaning visitor referred to Hazel as 'she', the guinea pig mother had shifted from tolerance to anxiety. Hundreds of Chestnut-Hazel replicas was a visually appealing but otherwise worrying spectre, as it would certainly eliminate all possibility of parent and piglets achieving quality time.

'Why,' she asked, 'do you think Hazel is a she?'

The visitor had looked surprised. 'But she, er, he, looks like a girl!'

It was true. Hazel was so delicately built, so entrancingly blonde, and so demure under his long eyelashes, that he looked like a piggy princess. Give him a crown, a tutu, and a wand, and he'd be the Fairy Hazel. A very girly fairy.

'And,' said the visitor, 'she, er, he, has a girl's name.'

Did nobody read *Watership Down* when they were young? thought Merridy. But she exercised her patience, and did not roll her eyes at yet another display of literary ignorance. Perhaps, she thought, (for she had grown up in Africa), *Watership Down* hadn't made it this far east, and Australians were just brought up on Skippy.

Merridy made an inspection. 'I beg your pardon,' she said to the Fairy Hazel. The Fairy Hazel watched her with his eyes half-closed under his demure eyelashes. Merridy lifted him up and peered underneath his bottom. She couldn't see anything obvious. Merridy put Hazel down and he looked at her with a where-is-my-fresh-morning-grass sort of look. It was a long-suffering look. Merridy was getting used to the long-suffering look, but it still made her jump to attention.

'Excuse me a minute,' she had said to the surprised visitor, running down the fire escape to pick fresh morning grass. She was disturbed by Hazel's lack of visible apparatus.

At least the case of the Mongrel Chestnut was clearcut. He was a straightforward pig. He was a what-you-see-is-what-you-get pig. He had no wiles. If Chestnut was anxious, he looked anxious. This was most of the time. If Chestnut was happy, he looked happy, with an anxious tinge, just in case of surprises.

Chestnut had no long-suffering get-me-grass stares, or bored how-can-she-be-so-stupid glances. And everyone called Chestnut 'he'.

Merridy, returning with a sizable sheaf of fresh morning grass, had decided a comparison was in order. 'Sorry, my boy,' she said to the Cherub Chestnut, who was about to launch into a mouthful. Chestnut, who always expected nasty surprises, was unsurprised. Merridy lifted him up and peered beneath his abundant rump. It would not be accurate, she thought, to describe Chestnut as 'well hung', but there was definitely a small bulge.

And so when Hector Protector popped the 'how-can-you-tell-that-Hazel-is-a-boar' question, Merridy's anxiety took a turn for the worse.

'The breeder said so,' she said defensively. 'Why, do you think he is not a boar?'

'No no,' said Hector Protector, 'I'm sure the breeder is right, but I wondered how you tell a girl pig from a boy pig.'

'In the usual way, apparently,' said Merridy. And she picked the Cherub Chestnut up from under his newspaper to demonstrate.

'Aha,' said Hector Protector. The Cherub Chestnut looked as if he was about to be spitted for a Peruvian barbecue, in other words, panicked. Merridy put him down quickly to relieve his panic. She lifted the Angel Hazel into the air to give Hector Protector a clear view.

'Hmm,' said Hector Protector. 'Hazel must be too young for detectable equipment.'

'But I'm sure he'll grow into it,' he added, noting the anxious vibe emanating from the guinea pig mother.

Hazel stared unfazed at his bearded visitor, as a strip of newspaper disappeared steadily between his adorable pink lips.

Merridy kept her nephew up to date with guinea pig events by telephone. 'Hazel and Chestnut,' she said, 'are now eating grass, dandelions and white lawn daisies.'

'Do they like pumpkin?' asked Alexander Scott, who was comparatively expert when it came to guinea pig fodder. 'It has tons of Vitamin C.'

'Yes,' said Merridy, 'but they won't eat capsicum. Which also has tons of Vitamin C.'

'Nor will I!' giggled Alexander, squirming with revulsion.

'Never mind,' said Merridy, 'nor did I, until I grew up. Then my taste buds changed.'

'Maybe Hazel and Chestnut's taste buds will change,' said Alexander. 'But mine won't!'

Merridy laughed.

'When will they grow up and have babies?' said Alexander Scott.

'No babies,' said Merridy. 'Remember, they are both boys!'

'Oh,' giggled Alexander, 'I forgot. Because Hazel is a girl's name!' He collapsed in paroxysms of mirth, dropping the telephone loudly on the kitchen floor.

Oh dear, thought Merridy. She waited for Alexander Scott to retrieve his breath, and the telephone.

'It is also a boy's name,' she explained. 'He's named after a famous boy-rabbit hero called Hazel, from a famous book called *Watership Down*.'

But she felt uneasy. Had she unwittingly inflicted Hazel with an identity crisis? Was this why he had no balls? Would he still grow them if he thought he was a girl? Did it matter?

'Yes!' she said firmly, 'Hazel is a boy! And Chestnut is a boy, which means he cannot make Hazel pregnant, which means I will not have hordes of Chestnut-Hazel babies and be eaten out of house and home. Two babies is quite enough!'

'Aaah nooo!' lamented Alexander Scott, who thought it was

a fine idea that his aunty be eaten out of house and home by hordes of guinea pig babies.

Just to be absolutely certain, Merridy checked her new guinea pig manual, which she had bought because it was a lot shorter than Google. She had checked it several times already, but she checked again in case there was something she had missed.

'Sexing guinea pig babies is not an easy task,' she read. Well, that was stating the obvious. 'It is best left to the experts,' she read on. The manual did not advise on what to do in the absence of such experts. There followed a brief and inadequate explanation of male and female guinea pig parts, with an unhelpful diagram.

She picked up Chestnut again and peered under his bottom. It looked the same as usual. Chestnut's eyes popped, as usual. 'Sorry my boy,' she said, and gently put him down. Hazel gave her a warning glare, which she ignored. 'It's important for me to check,' she told him, 'because I don't want to be giving you an identity crisis!' And she picked him up. There was, as usual, nothing to be seen. Not a bump, not a bauble, not a sausage. Absolutely nada.

Hazel was a pig with no balls.

And in a pedigree cream boar this was a serious omission.

6

Another unsettling question

THE ARRIVAL OF HAZEL AND CHESTNUT had caused a stir in the local vicinity, and by the end of the second week of visitors and their relentless stream of queries, Merridy was wrung out. It was as exhausting as being teacher to an excitable kindergarten class, except that her pupils were all ages and sizes and did not go home at three o' clock. Fortunately the deluge was abating, because the guinea pig mother's reserves of patience were wearing thin. To her mind it was understandable in a kindergarten-age person to ask a lot of repetitive questions and want to touch and squeeze and poke the object of interest, but what was less easy to comprehend was how certain mature-age persons behaved when it came to the matter of small defenceless rodents. It was also aggravating when such persons behaved in a tactless and overbearing manner toward the mother of such rodents. Flattery and adulation did not excuse such behaviour, she thought.

For another recurrent question was beginning to bother her. She ignored it, but it lurked like a persistent white elephant.

'It's one thing for me to make an inspection,' said Merridy to the guinea pig grandmother on the telephone, 'because I am their mother and I have a responsibility. But it is quite another,' she said, 'for a random and ignorant hamster-enthusiast to make an inspection without so much as a "may I" or a "thank you", and to prod my guinea pigs' bottoms while doing so!'

The guinea pig grandmother made appropriately indignant noises.

'It's as if they see the guinea pigs as public property, or ornamental entities,' said Merridy. 'But Hazel and Chestnut are acutely intelligent sentient beings with individual sensitivies!' It was true. Hazel was acutely intelligent, and Chestnut had many individual sensitivities. He was individually sensitive to noises and humanoid monsters, for example.

'Oh yes, Hazel is very intelligent!' agreed the guinea pig grandmother enthusiastically. She had not yet met the Angel Hazel but was expert at judging intelligence, even from hearsay.

'He is indeed,' said Merridy.

She did not mention the lurking white elephant.

It was a relief when Hector Protector came to visit, because he did not ask repetitive questions and was a useful consultant. And he brought chocolate.

'Perhaps,' she said to Hector Protector as she peeled the foil off a stick of almond nougat Toblerone, 'it's like pregnant persons. All and sundry think the pregnant belly is available for personal comment, fondling and prodding, as if it is not attached to a person who might not want to be fondled and prodded.'

Hector Protector nodded. He was fondling and prodding the Angel Hazel on his knee, and the Angel Hazel was making approving musical sounds because he wanted to be fondled and prodded. He liked being prodded under the armpits, because it made him squeak.

'And otherwise perfectly polite people who would never dream of poking an unpregnant person in the belly and commenting on their weight, think it is fine to do so in that context,' said Merridy. She offered Hector Protector the Toblerone stick, then broke off a piece for herself and ate it.

Hector Protector nodded in agreement. 'Spot on,' he said, and, 'What are you doing with all this food?'

'Offerings,' said Merridy, 'to the Angel Hazel and the Cherub Chestnut. Would you like an iceberg lettuce?' She was sorting an array of culinary gifts into categories for distribution around the neighbourhood. Well-meaning supplicants had brought diverse offerings for the guinea pigs, including three iceberg lettuces, a bag of peanuts and a box of sugar lumps. Someone had contributed several tins of cat food, and Merridy had refrained from explaining that guinea pigs were neither feline nor carnivorous, because one must not look gift horses in the mouth, even if they are cat food. Another person had contributed dog biscuits, which was kindly but ill-considered.

Hector Protector sucked on his Toblerone and looked perplexedly at the tins of cat food. 'Thank you,' he said.

'This is unsuitable guinea pig fodder,' explained Merridy. 'Iceberg lettuce gives them the runs, peanuts are for monkeys, and sugar lumps are for horses. I'm surprised somebody did not bring them birdseed!' She laughed. 'But there were also numerous carrots, apples and bags of grass, which the guinea pigs have eaten!'

In fact, Chestnut was still eating the most recent bag of grass, with a somewhat desperate air. He was gobbling as much as he could while the Angel Hazel was being fondled.

And then the lurking white elephant manifested from an unexpected quarter. 'How long do guinea pigs live?' asked Hector Protector idly, tickling Hazel behind his perfect rose-petal ears.

The guinea pig mother coughed loudly. She distracted Hector Protector by offering him a raspberry smoothie, and herself by making it.

The question of guinea pig longevity was even more unsettling than the how-can-you-tell-that-Hazel-is-a-boar question, Merridy thought. For she had only just adopted her baby guinea pigs and was not ready to think about their eventual demise. It was disquieting when a well-meaning but thoughtless hamster-enthusiast remarked that 'the lifespan of a hamster is not very long.' Did visitors, Merridy pondered, to the parents of newborn humans ask tactless questions such as 'when is your baby going to cark it?' She thought not. In any case, she was convinced that guinea pigs would be much longer-lived than hamsters, which were more on a mouseish scale. And besides, Hazel and Chestnut belonged to an exceptionally long-lived family, and that was bound to rub off. It was ridiculous to be thinking about her cream boar and her handsome mongrel in their coffins. Merridy quickly dismissed a tragic image of Hazel and Chestnut lying wizened and lifeless on their deathbeds, with two tiny wheelchairs alongside.

But after a particularly harrowing dream in which the Angel Hazel was run over by a Volkswagen beetle at a petrol pump, Merridy decided to confront the matter head-on. She would consult her manuals, and Google, and persons who had experience with guinea pigs. And that night, she mentioned the white elephant to her mother. 'People keep asking me how long guinea pigs live,' she said, 'and I'm tired of people telling me that they don't live very long, and that I'll suffer because they'll die young, and that I ought to have found myself another species of companion!'

'Oh no!' said the guinea pig grandmother, sounding stricken. 'How long *do* they live?' she enquired anxiously.

'That,' said Merridy, 'I intend to find out.'

Merridy's research was expert and thorough, and threw up pleasing results. It confirmed that guinea pigs live much longer that might be expected of a small rodent. And a typical guinea pig certainly lives much longer than a typical mouseish hamster. And, better still, the lifespan of domestic guinea pigs far exceeds that of wild guinea pigs, because potentially fatal ailments tend to be nipped in the bud.

'Five to eight years on average,' said Merridy to the guinea pig grandmother, 'and some sources say eight to ten years. In domestic situations, because potentially fatal ailments tend to be nipped in the bud.'

The guinea pig grandmother heaved a sigh of relief, because she had been haunted recently and suddenly with a vision of four tiny coffins lined up ready for the grandpigs, and it had been most upsetting.

'And,' said Merridy triumphantly, 'they can live even longer!' Grass-roots enquiries had revealed a neighbouring household accommodating a venerable female guinea pig of impressive age. 'A twelve-year-old guinea pig lives around the corner!'

'Twelve years old!' exclaimed the guinea pig grandmother.

'Yes,' said Merridy. 'I met the neighbour, who was very friendly. But I did not meet the guinea pig, because she is arthritic and does not like visitors.'

A charming picture flashed into Merridy's head of the Angel Hazel and the Cherub Chestnut at her fiftieth birthday party. They were wearing party hats and looking slightly grizzled but otherwise hale and hearty. They were going on for eleven years old, which pleased the guinea pig mother greatly. Her guinea pigs would live long and healthy lives, into a grand old age, and be her faithful companions for years to come.

And it was true that Chestnut and Hazel belonged to an exceptionally long-lived family. The most exceptionally long-lived family member was Old Grandpa, who was ninety-seven years old. And because of Old Grandpa being so extremely old, everyone else in the family was young. For instance, Young Grandpa was sixty-eight years young. He was a champion swimmer with an entire room full of medals. His medals lined the pelmets and decorated a large noticeboard above the desk and filled numerous drawers and trunks and trinket boxes on the bookcases and under the bookcases and inside his filing cabinet. Young Grandpa had cut all the ribbons off his medals to save space. That's how much of a champion he was. And he was still winning medals, which was testimony to his youthfulness.

Then there was the guinea pig grandmother, who was sixty-six years young. She was a fast runner with long toes. The guinea pig grandmother would become famous as the Wallaby Whisperer of Cataract Gorge, photographed by thousands of Japanese tourists as she stalked wallabies up and down the rocky reaches feeding them homeopathic remedies for their ailments. But right now she was still working up to it. She had grandpigs to worry about, and a rambunctious grandson.

The rest of the family were spring chickens. There was Merridy, the guinea pig mother; and Alexander Scott's mother, whom he kept on her spring-chickenish toes; and Alexander Scott's uncle, who was trotting the globe with spring-chickenly abandon. Alexander Scott was the newest and most exuberant spring chicken.

And on the family age-scale, the babies Chestnut and Hazel were barely hatched. Chestnut was the hatchling second from the bottom. And the hatchling Hazel was absolute bottom. He was hardly even an egg. But for a hardly-an-egg-absolute-bottom pig, Hazel's intellect was advanced. And while the existence of his male apparatus might be in question, the existence of his ego was not. He was a precocious pig-egg, and an egg-head pig with a superior ego.

Merridy looked at her precocious egg-pig, and Hazel stared back at her with a what-did-you-expect stare. And she looked at the hatchling Chestnut, whose ego needed encouragement. She felt pleasantly relaxed, for she had put the lurking white elephant out to pasture and was satisfied that her chosen companions, the Angel Hazel and the Mongrel Chestnut, would be by her side for years to come. Which was plenty of time for Hazel to grow visible apparatus, and for Chestnut to grow his ego and become a confident, laid-back pig.

Merridy prepared her lines for subsequent commentary regarding guinea pig longevity. 'Guinea pigs are not ordinary rodents, you know,' she would say airily, and 'Up to twelve years in a domestic situation,' and 'Exponentially longer than hamsters'. She would put the nay-sayers in their places, the ones who suggested that guinea pigs were unsuitable companions based on an apparently inconsequential lifespan.

She practised on Hector Protector, who understood the interplay of nature and nurture. 'Guinea pig genes,' she explained, 'give them a head start in the rodent world. And domestic guinea pigs live even longer, because potentially fatal ailments are nipped in the bud.'

Hector Protector looked impressed when Merridy described the venerable but arthritic guinea pig around the corner. 'And because you will nip all such ailments in the bud, Hazel and Chestnut will probably live to twelve years and beyond,' he said, which was the right thing to say to a new guinea pig mother.

'Yes,' agreed Merridy, 'and because they belong to an exceptionally long-lived family, that is bound to rub off.'

'Excellent,' approved Hector Protector. 'All environmental influences are in their favour.' And he tickled the hatchling Chestnut on the tiny bald spot in the middle of his rosette, because it was the only part of his head still showing. The hatchling

Chestnut was hiding between his mother's kneecaps, or thought he was.

The almost-egg pig Hazel snoozed virginally in his hay. He looked as innocent as a lamb, and like a small furry deity in a manger.

7

The proper care of guinea pigs

WITH THE QUESTION OF GUINEA PIG LONGEVITY SHELVED and the matter of baubles swept neatly under the carpet, Merridy settled comfortably into her new role as guinea pig mother. And Hazel and Chestnut settled comfortably into Green Street. They loved their pink sparkly indoor box, and Merridy erected a chickenwire-covered playpen in the garden for daytimes. She looked up 'guinea pig accommodation' and found handy hints, such as 'how to make a pigloo out of an old ice-cream container'. Chestnut's pigloo was blue, and Hazel's was white. Each had a doorway cut into one side and, turned upside down, they made excellent shelters. In Hobart, with the mountain liable to chuck down snow and rain in all seasons, this was very important.

Merridy shopped at the local pet shop for a water bottle, the kind that attaches to chickenwire with a sipper spout on the end. She taught the guinea pigs how to drink out of the sipper spout. They were intelligent guinea pigs and caught on at once.

Each morning Merridy put dry food into the new guinea

pig food bowl, which is to say, guinea pig muesli. It looked like human muesli, but with fewer raisins and more roughage.

You could tell that the new food bowl was for guinea pigs because of the picture on the bottom. When the guinea pigs ate up all their muesli, there was a surprise waiting – a guinea pig head grinning up from the bottom of their clean bowl. It looked a bit crazy. Hazel ignored the crazy guinea pig head. Chestnut ate his muesli three-quarters down so he wouldn't get a fright.

Chestnut and Hazel now enjoyed an extensive menu of guinea-pig friendly foods. Newspaper wasn't on the official list, but was obviously thrilling to guinea pig tastebuds and made a pleasing sound when shredded. Merridy was unsure about the ink content and paper ingredients, but it was satisfying to see irritating politicians shredded into compostable matter.

Then there was weetbix. Weetbix wasn't on the official list either, but it was packed with fibre and as good as prunes for the digestion. Weetbix complemented the guinea pig muesli nicely. 'Morning boys!' trilled Merridy in the mornings when she got out of bed. 'Weetbix!' Hazel and Chestnut knew that tone and would raise their sleepy heads in readiness to pounce.

Guinea pigs made for an earth-friendly household, Merridy discovered. If Merridy ate a banana, the pigs devoured the skin. If Merridy cooked pumpkin soup, the pigs sucked up the peel. If Merridy chewed an apple, the boys consumed the core. It was a well-balanced arrangement. Furthermore, guinea pig pellets could be laid on the vegie patch to encourage a fine growth of organic vegies. Merridy hadn't got to the vegie patch stage, but all in good time. She was busy educating and feeding the Angel Hazel and the Cherub Chestnut, and the vegie patch could wait.

After breakfast, Merridy carried the guinea pigs down the fire escape to their playpen. The guinea pigs grazed on the grass until it was as flat and smooth as a marsupial lawn, and then Merridy moved the playpen to a new patch. Luckily for the guinea pigs, the autumnal rains kept the grass growing faster than they could eat it.

If it was a pleasant day Merridy gardened while the guinea pigs grazed. She was working on a selection of herbs and pansies in pots. The herbs would be nutritious and delicious and the pansies would look pretty next to the playpen. As she gardened, she observed the guinea pigs' habits and routines, because she was gathering data on guinea pig behaviour. 'As a guinea pig mother, it is my duty to be informed!' she declared.

Hazel watched his mother coolly as she dug about with a trowel and lugged a watering can back and forth. He was observing his mother's habits and routines.

Chestnut's habits tended towards the furtive. He preferred to eat in private inside his pigloo. The pigloo moved about like a headless blue turtle when Chestnut moved to a new patch of fodder.

Hazel preferred to eat in the open, using his pigloo for cosy naps. Hazel's habits were surprisingly bold and self-serving for a pig so small and angelic.

Who would have thought, contemplated Merridy as she took a break on the rickety swing seat, that two guinea pigs could be so different in personality and bearing. Where Chestnut was fearful, Hazel was unfazed. Where Chestnut was anxious, Hazel was poised. Chestnut ate with gusto, and Hazel ate with restraint.

Merridy didn't know that Hazel would one day be gluttonously unrestrained and develop impressive love handles. She pushed herself meditatively back and forth on the swing seat, soaking up the midday sun. But her meditation did not last, for Hazel issued a pointed pick-me-long-grass-at-once instruction, and she hurried off to pick it from beneath the still-burgeoning rose bush. Hazel was training his mother, and she was turning out an excellent student. She stuffed the long grass through the chickenwire towards Hazel's pink lips.

In the evenings Merridy brought Hazel and Chestnut up the fire escape and into the bright and colourful kitchen of her eyrie. It was a cosy time of day, and the lava lamp's golden globules rose up and down with rhythmic somnolence as twilight deepened and the wide window darkened to deepest blue. Merridy cooked her dinner quickly, because she was a fan of efficient cooking, and Chestnut ate the skins and ends of the vegies quickly, because he was a fan of efficient eating. 'Chestnut Pink-Foot Little Chomper Pugh!' said Merridy fondly. 'You are an eating machine.'

Hazel was an eating machine in his own way, and was ingesting newspaper spaghetti. 'Nothing goes to waste in this household,' said Merridy. She tossed a handful of green bean ends into the pink sparkly box. Hazel chewed a tasty scrap of green bean daintily but thoroughly. 'Except onion peels,' she added, because guinea pigs did not eat onions. They did not eat potato peelings either, but Merridy ate her own potato peels. 'They are the most nutritious part of the potato,' she said to Hazel and Chestnut as she grated tasty cheese onto a deliciously baked specimen, 'and besides, it's a waste of energy to peel a potato.' Chestnut had finished his green beans and was onto the carrot peelings. Merridy also thought it a waste of energy to peel a carrot, but she peeled them for Chestnut and Hazel. 'I'm surprised you don't get indigestion,' said Merridy to Chestnut, 'because you gobble your food so quickly.' Chestnut looked anxiously at his mother, as if she might steal the rest of his carrot peelings before he could gobble them. 'And I'm surprised you get enough to eat!' said Merridy to Hazel, 'because you eat much more slowly than

Chestnut!' Hazel chewed his final bean scrap thoughtfully. He was growing, but not as fast as Chestnut, whose rump continued its abundant expansion and was now three times larger than Hazel's petite hindquarters.

After dinner, Merridy sat at her Apple laptop writing restaurant reviews, or checking her email, and sometimes editing a tedious document, and sometimes editing a thrilling one. When it was time for hot chocolate, she released Hazel and Chestnut onto the hideously striped kitchen carpet for exercise. This meant a speedy dash by Chestnut under the nearest shelter, which was the kitchen table, and cavorting by Hazel, who relished his freedom. The guinea pigs were hard to catch, but it gave the guinea pig mother exercise too, and a great deal of amusement. Chestnut wanted to be caught at once, but leapt away in fright when his mother advanced. And Hazel didn't want to be caught at all, and wedged himself discreetly in obscure hidey holes. Once, Merridy found him wedged in an ugg boot.

At bedtime, Merridy shredded fresh newspaper for the pink sparkly box, and Hazel hopped for joy. Chestnut buried himself deeply in the fresh bedding. Merridy covered the box with a warm towel, to keep off Antarctic drafts, and left the box in the kitchen by the blue sparkly couch, because she slept better when Hazel wasn't shredding politicians in her left ear. 'Good night, my baby boys!' she called as she put on her pyjamas, 'Good night!'

And in her wide pink bed under the window, with the stars twinkling above her head, the guinea pig mother slept the sleep of the truly contented.

8

The foibles of *guinea piggus domesticus*

IT WAS ONE MONTH after the Hobart Guinea Pig Show, and Merridy felt she was becoming an experienced guinea pig mother. 'I now have three manuals about guinea pigs,' she announced to the guinea pig grandmother, per telephone as usual. 'I have *The Guinea Pig Owner's Guide*, and *The Proper Care of Guinea Pigs*, and *Your Very Own Guinea Pigs*.'

The guinea pig grandmother exhaled noisily, which made her sound impressed.

'They have dull titles,' said Merridy, 'but excellent photographs. And it's handy to look up something in a manual, like how to worm a guinea pig, and find one explanation, instead of five million Google recommendations.'

'Worms?' queried the guinea pig grandmother anxiously.

Merridy didn't answer. She was admiring the manuals, which were slim, succinct, orderly, and beautifully illustrated with photographs of guinea pig accessories and astonishing breeds of guinea pig.

'Did you know,' said Merridy to the guinea pig grandmother, 'that guinea pigs are called pocket pets?'

'But they have no pockets,' objected the guinea pig grandmother, who was an expert on pocketed species, like wallabies, wombats and potoroos.

Merridy laughed. 'It's because they are pocket-sized,' she said. 'They fit into human pockets.'

It was true. Chestnut and Hazel fitted perfectly into the pockets of her fluffy green dressing gown. They enjoyed being in her pockets, especially Chestnut, because he felt safe.

'The guinea pigs graze their grass smooth and flat,' said Merridy to the guinea pig grandmother, 'like a marsupial lawn. But they have no pockets, so it's a pseudo-marsupial lawn!'

The guinea pig grandmother thought this was very witty.

The manuals were bursting with useful information on subjects like 'the importance of clipping your guinea pig's nails'. And so Merridy learned how to clip guinea pig nails, and a lot more besides. 'Make sure to snip the tips only and not to cut into the quick,' instructed *The Guinea Pig Owner's Guide*. Merridy tried to see the quick of a guinea pig's nail, so she did not hurt anypig. But she couldn't see any quick, on either Hazel or Chestnut. 'If your guinea pig kicks, use a towel papoose,' said the manual. There was a picture of a guinea pig in a towel papoose. It looked like a Native American baby with a furry face. Its front feet stuck out of the top, available for nail clipping. The back feet were hidden. The picture did not explain how to cut the back toenails. 'Perhaps you have to papoose the guinea pig's head end, to cut the back toenails,' speculated Merridy.

But Hazel and Chestnut made nail clipping easy. Hazel was bored stiff, and Chestnut was paralysed with fright. And so Merridy did not hurt anypig by accident.

Merridy learned how to weigh a guinea pig. She weighed Hazel and Chestnut on her fine-quality Swiss kitchen scales, for the sake of precision, and also because they did not budge the needle on the ordinary-quality Australian bathroom scales. They were much too light for ordinary bathroom scales. She squatted on the floor with the scales, so that anypig leaping accidentally out of them would not have far to fall.

'Weekly weighing,' she explained to Hazel and Chestnut, 'is important, because if you start to lose weight, it means something is wrong.'

'And it will help me nip any potentially fatal ailments in the bud,' she added, 'so that you live to a venerable and vigorous old age!'

At his first weigh-in, Hazel weighed a featherlight three hundred and sixty grams. He was now ten weeks old. Although he had grown, he was still a very petite boar. In fact, three blonde angels could have fitted comfortably into the weighing bowl.

At his first weigh-in, Chestnut weighed an impressive five hundred and eighty-two grams. He had spent a solid month eating, and was now four months old and expanding rapidly. 'You are a robust and healthy pig, Chestnut,' said Merridy, admiring his fine shiny haunches. 'And you have a robust and healthy appetite.' Chestnut filled up half of the weighing bowl, and looked as happy as a sailor in a coracle about to capsize at sea. Merridy lifted Chestnut out of the coracle and placed him on the hideously striped carpet to cheer him up. Chestnut lunged for the nearest available shelter, which happened to be up Merridy's left trouser leg. 'Ouch!' she squeaked, for Chestnut needed another nail clipping and his scrabbling was scratchy. Chestnut came to rest above Merridy's left ankle and she left him there for the moment. Chestnut didn't scrabble when he felt safe.

Merridy wrote down the guinea pig weights in her diary.

'You are almost twice the size of Hazel,' said Merridy to

Chestnut above her ankle. To be accurate, Chestnut weighed slightly less than twice the weight of the featherlight angel, but his bottom was three times the breadth of the angel's slender rear. 'I wonder,' she said to the slender angel, 'how big you will grow?'

It would have discombobulated all and sundry to imagine the slender angel becoming a Hazel-mammoth weighing one thousand four hundred and seventy-five grams.

'Did you know,' said Alexander Scott to his hippy aunty, 'that guinea pigs eat their own chocolate raisins?!' He cackled with glee. Choklit and Little Spot produced a great many chocolate raisins, and he did a great deal of cleaning up. But sometimes Choklit and Little Spot cleaned up their own chocolate raisins.

'Well,' said Merridy, 'I thought Chestnut was cleaning his, er, tail, yesterday, but then I noticed he was eating.' Neither event was in itself unusual, because the guinea pigs practised excellent personal hygiene, and Chestnut was always eating. But it had looked rather like a chocolate raisin, and Merridy did not give chocolate raisins to her guinea pigs. It was not on the list of guinea-pig friendly foods.

Alexander Scott exploded with mirth, and Merridy moved the telephone a bit further from her ear.

'They get them out of their bottoms!' he chortled.

And it was true. Merridy had researched this unusual behaviour, and discovered that Chestnut was not alone in producing his own snacks. 'Apparently it keeps their gut flora in equilibrium,' she said to Alexander Scott.

'What is gut flora?' snorted Alexander.

'And they produce two sorts of chocolate raisins,' continued Merridy, 'one sort which is good for compost, and the other sort which is good for digestion.'

'Hahaha,' laughed Alexander Scott.

'And gut flora,' explained Merridy, 'are microbes. If you have the proper sort they help digestion. We have them too. But guinea pigs need their own chocolate raisins to feed their proper flora.'

Alexander Scott hooted loudly. 'I'm glad we don't have to feed our proper flora!'

Hazel and Chestnut were expert at feeding their proper flora, and contorted nimbly into impressive yoga twists when extracting a chocolate raisin. It was an unusual foible, with a clean and green edge, since it involved recycling. And it required unusual dexterity, which one might not ordinarily expect of a comfortably rounded rodent.

The genus *guinea piggus domesticus*, Merridy discovered, had other unusual foibles.

For example, their legs might be twiddly and short, but they could exert astonishing force. Merridy discovered this repeatedly, because she was often trying to catch a guinea pig.

'Catching guinea pigs,' she said to Hector Protector, 'is an acquired skill.' Hector Protector was watching the Angel Hazel cavort on the hideously striped carpet. 'Try it,' said Merridy.

After several ineffectual lunges, Hector Protector stopped to wipe his brow. Hazel had cavorted from one end of the kitchen to the other and back again, and was having a whale of a time eluding his large bearded pursuer. He had a catch-me-if-you-can twinkle in his beautiful black eyes. Hector Protector pretended he had given up, and reached for the half-eaten stick of Toblerone on the kitchen table. Then he turned swiftly on his left heel and made a grab for Hazel's delicate haunches. He succeeded this time in making contact, upon which the Angel Hazel dug his pink feet into the carpet, and pushed. Merridy laughed out loud. It was absolutely astonishing that a diminutive guinea pig with ridiculously tiny legs could match a well-muscled six-foot humanoid monster for strength. Hazel had dug in his tiny pink heels, and wriggled his torso like a slippery fish. Hector Protector uttered a yelp, and let go, because it is almost impossible to hold onto a slippery fish with powerful pink heels.

'Guinea pig catching,' observed the guinea pig mother, 'requires the agility of an impala and the holding power of a bull terrier!'

It also required, in the case of the Angel Hazel, a spot of cunning.

There was no doubt that the Angel Hazel had wiles. It was hard to believe that a featherlight and diminutive furball with such innocent demeanour could be wily, but he was. 'Perhaps it's a trait peculiar to creams,' said Merridy to Hector Protector, 'because Chestnut hasn't a wily bone in his body.' Hector Protector was resting on the couch, reviving himself with a triangle of Toblerone. He was observing the wily Hazel, who had stopped cavorting to practise another of his favourite wiles, which was to let his looks do the talking. He sat perfectly still on the hideously striped carpet like a perfectly groomed princess in line for a beauty pageant. His tiny pink paws sat side by side beneath his creamy throat, his long eyelashes were lowered, and his pink lips pouted exquisitely beneath his heart-shaped pink nostrils. Then he looked up at his mother, his little pink mouth slightly open, and she caught her breath, for he was beautiful beyond description and utterly irresistible. Hector Protector observed the changing expression on Merridy's face, which had flitted from speculative to soppy in a matter of seconds.

'The Angel Hazel,' he remarked, 'has you round his little finger,' which was not strictly true, because Hazel had no little finger, but was metaphorically apt. The guinea pig mother looked pliant and, possibly, hypnotised.

Merridy stooped to pick up the wily princess, and Hazel let

her. Right now he wanted to be caught, and cosseted, and fed sprigs of something delicious, and so he rewarded her with a musical squeak. Hector Protector shook his head.

And then Merridy discovered another unusual foible of the genus *guinea piggus domesticus*, by accident, because it would not have occurred to her to try and hypnotise a *piggus*, and especially not the *piggus* Hazel.

Merridy laid the *piggus* Hazel on her lap, upside down with his creamy tummy exposed, all the better to feed him a sprig of something delicious. She patted his creamy forehead, and stroked his pink nose, and placed a warm palm over his beautiful black eyes. Whereupon Hazel threw his adorable head backwards and lay motionless. He looked like a corpse, with his legs sticking out straight and stiff. 'Hazel!' squeaked Merridy anxiously, 'are you all right?' Hazel lay like a *piggus* transfixed. His head felt heavy in her hand. It was unnerving, and Hector Protector sat up for a better look. Merridy lifted her hand to peer at the *piggus* Hazel's face, and the *piggus* Hazel twitched. He twisted his neck and looked at her reprovingly. Then he threw out a do-it-again-right-now stare. Merridy sighed with relief. She put her warm palm over Hazel's eyes and Hector Protector watched intrigued as Hazel threw himself backwards into corpse mode. 'It seems,' commented Hector Protector, who had studied hypnosis and was an expert on the subject, 'that you have hypnotised a guinea pig.' He did not mention that the *piggus* had first hypnotised Merridy.

The *piggus* Chestnut liked it too, because he couldn't see anything with his eyes covered. And so Merridy learned how to hypnotise a *piggus*.

The genus *guinea piggus domesticus* had other, less demanding foibles. When a *piggus* was sleepy, it lay curled on its side, and when a *piggus* was dreaming, its ears twitched. When a *piggus* was hungry, it wheeked loudly; and when a *piggus* was exploring, it chirruped special exploring noises.

And when a *piggus* was happy, it leapt into the air like a spring lamb. This was an endearing and hilarious foible. When Hazel and Chestnut were released into their playpen they kicked all four legs off the ground and tossed their heads in an excess of joy. They flexed their heels and wiggled their torsos and pronked like miniature short-legged springbok on their pseudo-marsupial lawn. 'Popcorning,' said *The Guinea Pig Owner's Guide*, 'is the technical expression for such happy hopping'. Merridy thought popcorns were one of the best things about *guinea piggus domesticus*.

Another best thing was the *piggus* hug. Because, like a *T. rex*, a guinea pig cannot hug with its arms. And so the species invented another sort of hug to express affection, which they do abundantly and with gusto. 'Guinea pigs hug with their heads!' exclaimed Merridy when she twigged to the insistent head nudging, and felt a distinct prickle behind the eyelids. A guinea pig head hug melted Merridy's heart every time without exception. If Hazel bestowed a head hug, she was putty in his hands, and when Chestnut offered one, she wanted to offer him a medal for bravery. It was even better than popcorning, the feel of a soft *piggus* head pushing into the palm of her hand, or nudging her under the elbow. 'And this is how I know you love me,' said the guinea pig mother fondly to her beloved baby boars.

9

Top pigs and bottom pigs

THE SINGLE THORN IN THIS PICTURE OF DOMESTIC BLISS came down to the still-missing pair of baubles. Perhaps that made it a dual thorn, thought Merridy, but whether single or dual, it was a downright nuisance. The thorny issue, thorn, or thorns, was and/or were inescapable, and Merridy felt a lurking uneasiness beneath her overall composure. She liked her life serene and orderly, and she liked explanations, and the missing baubles lacked adequate explanation and their absence inserted a note of uncertainty into the predictable order of things. Which is to say, that the guinea pig mother could not with absolute conviction state that Hazel was a boy. She could not be completely confident that he would not become a mother. And that was a bothersome possibility, which she did her best not to dwell upon.

'No,' said Merridy emphatically to herself in the bathroom mirror. 'I am not going to think about it!' And at once her brain was overrun with hordes of Hazel-Chestnut replicas. They chirped and wheeked and scampered about the inside of her skull, and made her feel helpless and, well, overrun. It was impossible to imagine the quantities of fodder that such a herd would gobble, and how many packets of muesli she would have to buy each week. 'Stop!' demanded Merridy loudly. Her cheeks were flushed. 'Walk!' she ordered. She found walking an excellent remedy for overrunning visions of this nature.

Hazel might not have been showing visible apparatus, but he was beginning to show metaphorical balls. It was unpleasant for Chestnut, who was used to having Hazel as a screen, a blanket and a shield, to have Hazel suddenly display such boarish behaviour. It gave him nasty surprises, and meant that he spent more time in his pigloo.

'Hazel!' remonstrated Merridy on one such occasion. Hazel had nipped Chestnut on his abundant rump, and Chestnut had shrieked and run into his pigloo. 'Naughty boy!' said Merridy to Hazel. Hazel felt pleased, having shown somepig he was boss, and his beautiful black eyes gleamed wickedly. Merridy felt somewhat disturbed, because virtuous blonde angels ought not to be bossy and wicked. She was not sure how to discipline a small bossy and wicked angel.

Merridy researched bossy behaviour, wondering if it would prove Hazel's masculinity, and whether it would offer disciplinary tips. *The Guinea Pig Owner's Guide* had a complete section dedicated to bossiness.

'You will observe,' she read, 'that there is a strict ranking order within a group of guinea pigs.' Merridy hadn't noticed, but perhaps two guinea pigs were not strictly a group. 'Two males cannot fit into this hierarchy, and so the reigning male must prove himself the stronger.'

'Oh dear!' she said, wondering if Hazel was trying to prove himself the reigning male, even if Chestnut was twice his size.

Or was Chestnut the reigning male, even though he was terrified? Why would a pair of guinea pig babies even need a reigning male?

'To prove his dominance,' she read, 'the stronger male threatens the weaker one by showing a wide-open mouth.' But Chestnut, thought Merridy, is the stronger male, and he only opens his mouth wide to eat. 'Or do they mean strength of character?' she pondered. It was possible that Hazel was a stronger character, because nothing unnerved his nerves, not even large bearded visitors.

'Ah!' said Merridy as she read on, 'Oh!' and 'Oh no!'

'This is one occasion where guinea pigs are tempted to bite,' instructed the manual. 'With hackles raised, they will grind their teeth noisily, and serious bites may occur.'

'Holy moly!' said the guinea pig mother, confronted with a spectre of nastily grinding teeth and bleeding wounds.

'Once the leader establishes dominance,' advised the manual, 'the weaker animal will be rejected by the tribe. He will not be allowed to eat, he will not find a place to sleep, and he must leave the tribe to make a new life.'

Merridy saw Chestnut wandering alone and friendless out in the Hobart winter rain, searching for a sheltering pigloo, and failing, and acquiring hypothermia and dying a miserable and lonely death of frozen starvation, with his abundant rump shrunken and emaciated. She shut off the vision quickly. 'Never!' she said, 'Never! I cannot believe the Angel Hazel or the Cherub Chestnut would ever behave so badly. No. They are gentle defenceless creatures, and placid, and besides, they do not live in a tribe, they live with me, and I will always find them a place to sleep and food to eat.'

Merridy closed *The Guinea Pig Owner's Guide* with a snap.

Bossiness displayed itself in curious ways. The downside was that her boars were becoming harder to manage. The upside of the displays was that Hazel was showing more and more bossy behaviour, which was typical of guinea pig boars, and which gave the guinea pig mother hope.

'Listen to this!' said Merridy to the guinea pig grandmother. She held the telephone down to the pink sparkly box, because a boarish engagement was in progress. Hazel was rumbling like a furry motorbike and wiggling his miniscule buttocks from side to side. He looked like a miniature blonde bull, and completely ridiculous. But the bottom-wiggling obviously looked alarming to Chestnut, who was on the back foot, so to speak, with the whites of his eyes showing. He held his nose high in a gesture of alarm. Suddenly Hazel lunged forward and their noses almost collided, but both he and Chestnut leapt up and backwards before they touched. Chestnut fell over his fine bottom, wheeked in consternation, and retreated under a pile of hay.

'Did you hear that?' exclaimed Merridy. 'Hazel was rumblestrutting!'

'What?' said the guinea pig grandmother.

'It's a specialist term for bossy behaviour in guinea pigs,' explained Merridy. 'It's dominance behaviour, which means Hazel is trying to prove himself the reigning male. He was rumbling and wiggling his bottom from side to side like a pacing bull!'

'But Hazel is the youngest!' exclaimed the guinea pig grandmother. 'If any pig is the reigning male, it should be Chestnut.'

'I know,' said Merridy. 'And then they did a guinea pig face-off,' she continued, 'and Chestnut lost.'

'Haha,' said the guinea pig grandmother. 'You mean a nose-up! I've seen Choklit and Little Spot do those. Little Spot wins because his nose is the longest.'

'A nose-up face-off!' giggled Merridy. 'The highest nose wins!'

'I'm surprised Hazel's nose was high enough,' said the guinea pig grandmother.

Merridy thought perhaps Chestnut's nose was dragged down by his abundant rump.

There was also prowling-and-growling, which Hazel did like a tiny blonde panther. He prowled up and down the pink sparkly box, growling musically. When Hazel prowled, Chestnut pretended he was invisible. When Hazel growled, the fur stood up on the back of his neck and he looked like a baby lion. It was hilarious, and seemed quite adorable to the guinea pig mother, even if it was neither to Chestnut.

And there was food-snatching. For instance, when Merridy tossed a breakfast weetbix in to Chestnut and one to Hazel, Hazel made a beeline for Chestnut's. He stole Chestnut's weetbix from under Chestnut's nose and dragged it into a corner where he guarded it fiercely like a Doberman Pinscher. Hazel made a funny, short-legged Doberman Pinscher. Luckily for Chestnut, he could eat Hazel's discarded weetbix, which he did at speed in case it too was snatched.

All in all, and despite his still questionable gender and angelic exterior, it seemed that Hazel was assuming the position of reigning male. Merridy hoped that once he had proven his status, he would settle back to being quiet and contemplative and leaving Chestnut in peace. 'Chestnut,' she said comfortingly to her handsome mongrel, 'I'm afraid that you are the bottom pig.'

Alexander Scott was hugely entertained by the notion of the tiny top-pig Hazel. 'Heeheehee!' he cackled, 'Hahaha!' When he had caught his breath sufficiently to hold a conversation, he said, 'Little Spot is my top pig. Because he has a longer nose.'

'So I've heard,' said Merridy. 'Hazel is my top pig even though his nose is smaller.'

'And,' she added, 'even though he has no balls.'

Alexander disappeared under the table. He had collapsed from an excess of hilarity. After a noisy hiatus, the expert guinea pig father asked an expert question. 'Does he chatter his teeth at Chestnut?' he wheezed. 'That means he wants to fight.'

'Hazel and Chestnut don't fight,' said Merridy, feeling relieved. It would be most unpleasant if her boars got into pigfights, because she was squeamish and not good with blood, and besides, she liked a peaceful and orderly life.

'Oooh,' sighed Alexander Scott, to whom pigfights were most appealing. Choklit and Little Spot only fought over food, which was funny in its own way, but not as exciting as a pigfight, he thought, hoping to see a proper one one day.

Fortunately Merridy could not foresee the immense complications that would result from future pigfights. She could not imagine the scrums and woundings and concussions, not to mention the enormous veterinary bills to come.

10

A momentous gathering

ON A FROSTY JULY MORNING the guinea pigs were listening to an excited telephone conversation. Which is to say, Hazel and Chestnut were listening to half of it in their pink sparkly box in Hobart, and Choklit and Little Spot were listening to the other half two hundred and seven kilometres further north and slightly west.

The conversation spanned the island that is Tasmania from top to bottom. At the southern end of the telephone was Merridy, the guinea pig mother, and at the northern end were the guinea pig grandmother and Alexander Scott.

The guinea pig grandmother was in a state of excitement. This in itself was not unusual. It's very exciting being a guinea pig grandmother. 'Hello!' she squeaked.

Alexander Scott was also excited, with two excited guinea pigs on his lap. 'How are Hazel and Chestnut?' he bellowed, but before Merridy could say, 'Hazel and Chestnut are fine, thank you,' he had grabbed the telephone and put the mouthpiece on

Choklit's flank. Now all Merridy could hear was a dark chocolate squeaking, which sounded as if it was inside a drain pipe.

Merridy put Hazel up to the phone and squeezed him. Hazel always squeaked to his grandmother on the phone, and he might as well squeak to Choklit. Sometimes it took a bit of squeezing, but usually he squeaked.

'We're coming to visit!' announced the guinea pig grandmother, who had retrieved the telephone. 'And!' she stopped. 'We are bringing Choklit and Little Spot!'

Hazel squeaked on, unmoved by this momentous news. Merridy cheered and gave Chestnut a fright. 'Sorry my boy!' she said, discarding the Angel Hazel and picking up the frightened Chestnut. She tried to squeak him into the phone, but Chestnut was too frightened to squeak. It would take a bit more squeezing to warm him up.

'We're coming for the whole weekend!' crowed Alexander Scott.

'Fantastic!' exclaimed Merridy. 'A guinea pig gathering! A guinea pig meet-and-greet! We'll have a guinea pig herd!' She looked at Hazel and Chestnut. 'Boys!' she announced. 'You're going to meet Choklit and Little Spot! They were our very first guinea pigs! They belong to your uncle, who is going to be a tramp-champ.'

Hazel looked indifferent and delved into the newspaper for a tasty morsel.

'And,' said Merridy, 'you'll meet your grandmother!'

Chestnut finally squeaked. It sounded a little forced, and like a squeaky door in need of oiling.

Merridy danced a little dance on the hideously striped kitchen carpet. All the best guinea pigs in the known universe would be gathered soon in her very own Green Street eyrie, in Flat Three! They would graze peacefully on the Green Street lawn in the daytime, and snuggle peacefully together at night. They would tear up twice as much newspaper and chew up twice as many irritating politicians. They would draw twice as many admirers and well-wishers. She stopped suddenly, at the thought of twice as many admirers and well-wishers. Perhaps she would keep the gathering a secret, to avoid such an influx. It would detract from the purpose at hand, and possibly scare Choklit and Little Spot, who had not travelled this far from home before, and might need a soothing environment.

'They're coming next weekend,' she said to the Angel Hazel and the Cherub Chestnut, 'and I must shop! More weetbix! Guinea pig muesli! Pumpkin! Pink ladies!' Hazel ignored his mother and chewed up the premier's nostril. Chestnut buried himself underneath a picture of a politician's substantial torso.

Merridy found a lime-green plastic box for the visitors. Well, for the guinea pig visitors. Alexander Scott would sleep in the queen-sized pink bed, and she and the guinea pig grandmother would sleep on the floor on comfy cushions.

'The lime green will set off Choklit's chocolate fur beautifully,' said Merridy, 'and complement Little Spot's orange colouring.' She liked colours to be arranged properly. She put old newspaper in the bottom of the lime-green box.

'Now!' she said happily to Hazel's demure eyelashes and Chestnut's expansive rump. 'We need two more pigloos. Little Spot and Choklit will need pigloos with bigger doorways. They are twice your size, Chestnut, and twice your size and a bit more, Hazel.' Chestnut pretended to be invisible, and Hazel bit a particularly offensive politician on the earlobe. 'I will have to empty two large containers of ice cream in four days. I will buy two litres of honeycomb with toffee bits, and two litres of vanilla bean with chocolate chips.' Chestnut's bottom wiggled. Hazel swallowed a tuft of politician hair. 'Those are the easiest to eat,' said Merridy, who had a sweet tooth, 'and I will have to eat five hundred millilitres of ice cream every day until Friday. Unless I have visitors.' She decided to invite Hector Protector for dinner right away, and added honeycomb and vanilla bean ice cream to her shopping list.

Two hundred and seven kilometres north and slightly west, the guinea pig grandmother stuffed a whole cauliflower into a bag. She liked to be well prepared. Old Grandpa was engrossed in a book in his special armchair, and outside, Young Grandpa weeded recalcitrant verbiage out of the cracks in the patio paving.

A little further down the beautiful Tamar Valley, Alexander Scott daydreamed about guinea pig meeting-and-greeting instead of doing his homework. His mother did not notice him gazing out of the window, because she was hanging pairs of slinky white trousers on the washing line. Alexander was going places in the trampolining arena, because he took after his gymnastical mother, but it was making her a lot of washing, because slinky white trousers showed a lot of dirt. Little Spot poked his furry nose out of the roosting box and Choklit dozed on a patch of white lawn daisies in an afternoon ray of winter sun. They did not know an important gathering was imminent.

Four days later Merridy woke with a start. Her pink bed felt cosy and from the kitchen she could hear the comforting sounds of waking guinea pigs. She peeked an eye above the windowsill and noted a dusting of snow on the mountain. 'Ugh,' she said. 'Snow.' Then she squeaked. 'Oh my guinea pig aunt – it's guinea pig meet-and-greet day!' This cheered her up immensely. She hopped out of bed, donned her green fluffy dressing gown and skipped into the kitchen. She took the warm towel covering off the pink sparkly box.

Hazel opened an eye. Even with one eye, he could throw a

stern look in his mother's direction. Merridy went to fetch the weetbix at once.

By eleven o'clock, the sun was out and the snow dusting had vanished from the top of the mountain. Merridy was delighted. It would soon be warm and dry enough to put the pigs out to play in their playpen. 'Now boys!' she instructed. 'The red igloo is for Choklit, and the green one is for Little Spot. No fighting!' She cut a large doorway into the side of Little Spot's igloo. The Angel Hazel and the Cherub Chestnut paid no attention. They were playing a chasing game under the newspaper. Chestnut, in an unusual burst of confidence, was playing the chaser. Hazel was playing the chasee.

The visitors were due any moment. Merridy set out morning tea. Chocolate biscuits for the human visitors. Carrot sticks and celery tops for the guinea pigs.

Chestnut caught Hazel and jumped on his back. He was in fine form for an anxious pig.

The sound of a car door alerted Merridy to the much-anticipated arrival. She hurried to the top of the fire escape. 'Wheek, wheek!' she called to the visitors. 'Wheek, wheek!' they shouted back. Merridy trotted down the steep metal steps. She could see Little Spot and Choklit in a cardboard box on the back seat of the car. Alexander Scott threw himself upon his hippy aunty, and squeezed her round the middle. 'Hello, tramp-champ!' huffed Merridy. Alexander Scott let go and leapt up the fire escape with gymnastical prowess.

The guinea pig grandmother gave Merridy a bunch of South African proteas from her garden. 'Guinea pigs eat protea leaves!' she announced. Proteas weren't on the official list of guinea-pig friendly foods, but by now Merridy wasn't surprised. Guinea pigs would eat pink ugg boots if they fancied.

Merridy followed the guinea pig grandmother upstairs, carrying the proteas and the cardboard box. Choklit looked particularly distinguished this morning with his smart white nose-stripe. Merridy tickled the tiny bald spot in the middle of his rosette. He had beautiful dark skin, the colour of shiny dark chocolate, and each of his beautiful dark hairs was tipped with copper that caught the light. Choklit was squeaking deep, dark chocolate squeaks.

Little Spot nosed his pointy nose about the cardboard box in search of protea leaves. With his pelt gilded in the sunshine and his ridge at attention and his liquid dark eyes, he looked absolutely ravishing. The tiny spot on his forehead was white as snow.

'Good morning Choklit and Little Spot!' said Merridy. 'Welcome to Green Street! Welcome to my eyrie!'

Alexander Scott was on his knees making soppy noises. He was looking at the Angel Hazel, and the Angel Hazel was looking at him. Chestnut had hidden underneath the newspaper. His expansive rump gave him away, however, and Alexander Scott tickled it.

'They are soooo cute!' exclaimed Alexander Scott. 'And they have such tiny chocolate raisins!' Alexander Scott was an expert on chocolate raisins and very observant. Merridy looked at the chocolate raisins in the pink sparkly box, which looked normal, and looked at the chocolate raisins in the cardboard box, which looked gargantuan. 'That's a lot of composting material,' she said.

Guinea pig meeting-and-greeting was a serious business requiring special preparations. The guinea pig manuals said so.

'On the plus side,' said Merridy to the guinea pig grandmother, 'all four pigs are boys, eliminating the need for contraception.' She switched the kettle on for morning tea. 'And on the minus side, all four pigs are boys.' This meant posturing and fighting was on the cards, but she did not go into detail, because Alexander Scott was halfway to plunging Chestnut enthusiastically into the cardboard box, and Chestnut looked about to have a heart attack.

'If you put them all together right away,' explained Merridy, having rescued the stricken Chestnut, 'they will have territorial arguments and probably fight.' Alexander looked hopeful. 'No,' said Merridy, 'we do not want pigfights. They need to be in separate compartments to start with, and sniff each other for a while first, and then, after a suitable length of time, when they have got used to each other, they can be introduced.'

'But we're only here for the weekend!' objected her nephew, imagining weeks of tedious sniffing.

'Yes,' said Merridy, 'so perhaps we'll speed up the introductions, but only after morning tea, and when they've got used to each others' scents.'

She brought over the lime-green box. 'This is the guest accommodation for Choklit and Little Spot,' she said. 'And these,' she indicated the two pigloos. The pigloos had taken a lot of hard eating, and Hector Protector had helped, but Merridy felt as if she would never eat a spoonful of ice cream again. She put the pigloos into the lime-green box, and Alexander Scott put in Choklit and Little Spot, who wheeked and whirred and walked in and out of the pigloo doorways. 'The pigloos,' said Merridy, 'are a success!'

The guinea pig grandmother was enchanted by the sight of her new grandpigs. She had the Angel Hazel on her lap. 'Oh,' she said to Merridy, 'isn't she adorable!' Merridy's eyes bulged slightly. 'He!' she said, pointedly.

The guinea pig grandmother hoisted Chestnut out from the pink sparkly box. Chestnut was relieved to be with Hazel again, but thoroughly alarmed by the new humanoid apparitions and the strange whirring guinea pigs. 'Oh!' cooed the guinea pig grandmother, 'look at your handsome crest!' Chestnut's rosette was a pristine snow-white, and he did look immensely handsome with his prize-winning crest and his fine round bottom. The guinea pig grandmother tickled the tiny pink bald spot in the middle of Chestnut's rosette. The new grandpigs, thought Merridy, are a success! It was turning out to be a very successful gathering.

The meeting-and-greeting was also a success.

To start with, the humans sat on the striped kitchen carpet with soft old towels on their laps. The towels were freshly washed, so they didn't smell of any particular pig. This was important for avoiding territorial squabbles.

Then the meeting-and-greeting began. The guinea pigs took turns on the soft towels. Two at a time, the humans held them close enough to sniff each other, but not close enough for sudden nipping. The guinea pigs sniffed and wriggled and revved like tiny motorbike engines.

'Can we put them all together?' begged Alexander Scott at intervals. 'Pleeeease!'

And eventually Merridy and the guinea pig grandmother decided it was safe for a whole-hog foursome.

The whole-hog foursome happened on Merridy's lap.

This was a great privilege.

The guinea pig mother carefully placed Choklit and Little Spot together with Hazel and Chestnut. Chestnut suddenly looked very small. Hazel looked like a midget. Little Spot and Choklit looked like walruses.

A cacophony of meet-and-greet pig-music broke out. It sounded like a guinea pig orchestra. Choklit was the double bass, with his deep chocolate rumbles. Little Spot was the tenor, with his medium-level grunting and an occasional squeal.

Chestnut offered a squeaky violinesque rendition, slightly off-key. And Hazel peeped musically in a high soprano.

The whole-hog orchestral foursome wiggled its four bottoms and strutted its sixteen short legs. It waved its pointy noses in the air. Little Spot dived ecstatically under Hazel's tummy, ousting Chestnut, who dived ecstatically under Choklit's rump. Little Spot looked ridiculous, like a tapir hiding under a mouse.

Merridy and the guinea pig grandmother were speechless with pride. Alexander Scott wriggled with merriment. Merridy sent her sister a text message. 'Guinea pig bliss,' she wrote, 'is a whole-hog foursome on my lap. Merridy-bliss is a lapful of guinea squeaks.'

11

A veterinary encounter

FLAT THREE SEEMED EMPTY AFTER THE VISITORS LEFT. Hazel and Chestnut did not make as much noise as a whole-hog foursome, and Merridy was left with a *piggus* duet instead of a *piggus* orchestra. And she missed her nephew's jollity and her mother's conversation. 'Boys,' she said to the guinea pigs in the evening as she stirred a pot of pumpkin soup on the stove, 'we are social animals, and we all need company.' The sky beyond the kitchen window was cobalt blue and studded with early evening stars. 'I'm glad of your company, Hazel and Chestnut,' she said, for without the sounds of chomping, rustling and squeaking, her eyrie would have been very quiet indeed.

Winters were long in Hobart, and trying, especially if you lived in an eyrie with Antarctic drafts. Merridy kept her fan heaters going and her fluffy green dressing gown handy, and stomped about in her pink ugg boots. She wore fingerless gloves at the Apple laptop.

It was Hazel and Chestnut's first winter. 'It's important to keep you snug,' said Merridy, having read that guinea pigs caught cold easily. She shredded extra newspaper into their pink sparkly box and put extraneous clothing items in for added warmth. Chestnut's favourite was a worn out beanie, into which he curled with his head covered and his rump blocking the doorway. Hazel preferred to mess about with a pair of old striped socks. First he chewed them, and then he lazed on them, and then he inserted himself into a sock and would not come out. Merridy picked up the sock, which looked like a striped python with a guinea pig inside it awaiting digestion. She bounced the python gently, but Hazel was happily wedged. 'I will leave you to it,' she said, 'but you may have to chew your way out.'

At bedtime Merridy filled three hot water bottles. She needed one for her feet and one for her tummy, and Hazel and Chestnut were small enough for one between them. She wrapped their hottie in a towel to prevent inadvertent chewing, for it would not do for the hottie to spring a leak.

Then Hazel acquired a skin problem. Nothing unsightly, but Merridy didn't want any guinea pig leprosy developing in the herd, especially not on her pedigree cream boar, so she took Hazel to the vet. A pocket-pet vet.

'Prevention is better than cure,' she said to Hazel as she popped him into the brand new black travel bag. The travel bag had a mesh window for views and air. It was a well-designed bag, with handles for carrying, and a zip. Merridy had bought it in case of visiting, or unexpected travel arrangements such as this one. She filled the bag with fresh grass to keep Hazel distracted, in case he was nervous of vets.

But Hazel wasn't nervous of anything. As she walked to the vet's, he swung gently back and forth in the travel bag like a genteel beachgoer in a comfortable hammock.

It was the guinea pig mother's first ever visit to a vet. She felt anxious, and curious, and proud, because she was taking a very fine specimen of the genus *guinea piggus domesticus* to a genuine pocket-pet specialist, who should know quality when he saw it.

Merridy spotted the vet surgery at once. There was a picture of a Shetland pony on the front door. Inside there was a waiting room, and behind a counter sat a nurse, who was attending to another patient. The other patient was inside a plastic cat carrier and looked small and hamsterish.

The nurse finished with the hamster patient and looked at Merridy. 'Good morning!' she said. 'Who do we have here?'

'Good morning!' said Merridy, and 'This is Hazel.' She let the nurse inspect Hazel inside his travel bag. 'Isn't she gorgeous!' said the nurse. Hazel eyed his new admirer with speculation. He knew ignorance when he saw it.

'Hazel,' said the nurse, writing down his name on a white card. 'Surname?'

'Pugh,' said Merridy. She spelled it out: 'P-U-G-H,' because even good spellers had difficulties spelling the surname 'Pugh'. It was Welsh, with a silent 'g', and caused a lot of mispronunciation.

'Pugh,' repeated the nurse, 'P-U-G-H.' She wrote down Hazel's details. 'Guinea pig, female, blonde.'

'Male,' said Merridy, who felt obliged to correct the nurse. 'He is named after the boy-rabbit hero in the children's classic *Watership Down*,' she added, not wanting the nurse to feel foolish. The nurse looked blank. 'Five months old,' added Merridy quickly, 'six hundred grams. Scaly in patches.'

Merridy and Hazel sat down in the waiting room. Merridy sat on the wooden bench, and Hazel sat inside the travel bag on her lap, watching through its window with a grass blade hanging from his pink lips.

The waiting room was full of photographs. Sausage dogs, and bull terriers, and fluffy kittens, and blue budgies, and even a belted Galloway. Merridy wondered if the vet had Shetland ponies and belted Galloways coming into the surgery through the front door. They would be a tight fit, especially the belted Galloway. Merridy looked for a guinea pig photograph, but couldn't find one. A pocket-pet vet ought to have loads of guinea pig photographs, she thought. But she spotted a guinea pig manual in the bookcase, and took it out.

A large and boisterous labrador came into the waiting room, panting and drooling and pulling on her owner's lead. 'It's all right, Hazel,' whispered Merridy tenderly, tickling his forehead. But Hazel watched the labrador boldly.

Merridy found a picture of some guinea pigs sitting on little carpets in a guinea pig show. One was labelled 'Pedigree Cream Boar' and looked like Hazel. But the vet called out before she could read any more. 'Hazel Pugh!' he called in a kind voice. 'Do come in!'

The pocket-pet vet had a long white beard. He crooned and fussed over Hazel, and told him how cute he was, and his beard brushed lightly across the top of Hazel's back. Hazel lapped it up as if he were in for a beauty treatment.

Excellent bedside manner, thought Merridy, who was impressed. 'He's a pedigree cream boar,' she said proudly. 'I bought him at the Hobart Guinea Pig Show.'

'A handsome fellow!' said the vet. He did not comment on Hazel's lack of male apparatus, and so Merridy did not mention it. He examined Hazel's pink skin with a magnifying glass, and peered at the scaly patches. 'I can't see any mites,' he said, 'which is good news. It could be a skin fungus.' Merridy felt relieved and alarmed at once. She did not like the idea of Hazel cultivating a skin fungus.

'I will take a little skin scraping,' said the vet, and stood up to find a scraping instrument. Merridy held tightly onto Hazel's hips in case he made a dash for freedom, but Hazel waited passively for the next stage of his beauty treatment.

Merridy left the vet with special guinea pig shampoo and a somewhat lighter wallet. But she was pleased. Hazel needed a shampoo and blow-dry for his scaly patches, and the vet would see if the skin scraping grew anything significant, like skin fungus. If it did, it just meant a lot more shampooing.

'And Chestnut will also need shampooing,' said Merridy to the travel bag, 'just in case.'

And so Merridy learned how not to bath a guinea pig. For Hazel and Chestnut did not enjoy being bathed. Perhaps pocket pets are allergic to being wetted, she concluded, even with special guinea pig shampoo.

Chestnut went first. 'Because you're an anxious pig,' said Merridy, 'and it's better to get it over with.' Chestnut sprang instantly out of the basin and landed on his mother's chest. It was astonishing how high Chestnut could jump in an emergency. Merridy lowered Chestnut a second time into the warm but not-too-hot water, and he sprang out a second time. He was an agile pig when stirred, and was making his mother soggy. 'Third time lucky,' said Merridy as she gripped his haunches firmly with one hand and squeezed a blob of shampoo out with the other. She rubbed it over Chestnut's abundant rump. Chestnut's eyes popped and he scrabbled for traction. Merridy sloshed water about for a rinse, but Chestnut was wet and slippery and shot out of the basin a third time.

'At least you are clean,' said Merridy, who was now dripping. She papoosed Chestnut in a towel from which his head protruded. His eyes bulged with fright. 'I'm sorry, Chestnut,' said

Merridy gently, and popped him on the couch with a pile of strategically placed comfort food. Then she turned to the Angel Hazel. A shredded politician hung from Hazel's lips like a party streamer. Merridy avoided his eye, which had a don't-you-dare-put-me-in-that sort of look. She put him in the basin with his party streamer.

Afterwards, Merridy added chocolate to the available comfort food, for herself. Her fluffy green dressing gown was sodden, and she had a bandaid on her forearm, for the Angel Hazel had protested strenuously and kicked. He had hurtled out of the basin like a blonde torpedo and landed with a thud on the bathmat. It had been stressful in the extreme, but there were no obvious injuries beyond her own, which was a tremendous relief.

Hazel had gotten away with a plain rinse, because his mother could not get to the shampoo. He was officially disgusted.

'Thank heavens,' said Merridy to the guinea pig grandmother, 'they didn't mind the blow-drying.' She had gingerly tested the effects of hot air on the drenched guinea pigs and it had been a success. The pleasantly roaring breeze had lulled Chestnut and Hazel into a fluffed-up stupor. 'Even Chestnut relaxed,' said Merridy, 'and I think Hazel has forgiven me.'

'But what about the skin fungus?' asked the guinea pig grandmother.

'Well,' said Merridy, 'there may not be one. The pocket-pet vet is going to see if Hazel's skin scraping grows anything.'

'I hope it doesn't,' said her mother, 'because you can't shampoo him!'

'Perhaps he just has scaly winter skin,' said Merridy hopefully, 'like me. Perhaps he just needs a moisturiser.'

The Angel Hazel lay fluffed up on the blue sparkly couch, his little pink paws tucked under his fluffed-out tummy. His eyes were half closed, and he looked golden and pristine in the lamplight. It was hard to believe he could be cultivating a skin fungus.

12

The bottom-sniffing fiasco

IT WAS ALMOST SPRINGTIME, and the mountain was obliging the residents of Hobart with a week of balmy, blossom-scented weather. This was just as well, because the Green Street residence had visitors again, and good weather helped regulate the visitors' activities. It was easier to keep the visitors outdoors than indoors.

The Originals were staying with the Young Ones for a whole ten days. Alexander Scott and the guinea pig grandmother had visited again briefly, but the Ridgeback Little Spot and the handsome Choklit were staying on.

It was proving to be a trying time for the guinea pig mother, because the Originals and Chestnut were being trying. They were trying out what it was like to do a guinea pig conga line, led by the Angel Hazel. The Angel Hazel was being congalined to distraction, and his immaculate golden pelt was being messed up.

'Bottom-sniffing,' said Merridy to her mother, the guinea pig grandmother, on the telephone. 'There's a lot of bottom-sniffing.'

The guinea pig grandmother made startled noises.

'And only one bottom is being sniffed,' said Merridy.

It was true. Choklit and Little Spot and even Chestnut, who had found a reservoir of courage now that he had moral support, were crowding around the Angel Hazel's still-delicate rump. They sniffed it and jumped on his back. They sniffed some more and pushed it around. They pushed each other out of the way, all the better to sniff. 'It's a bottom-sniffing frenzy,' said Merridy, observing the frenzy through the kitchen window.

'Do you think it's normal?' asked the guinea pig grandmother in alarm. She placed great faith in the virtues of normalcy. 'Perhaps you should ask the vet?'

'I googled it,' said Merridy in a resigned tone. Her manuals were uninstructive regarding the matter of bottom-sniffing, but Google had been copious in its assistance.

'It's either dominance behaviour, or the behaviour of boars on the loose,' sighed the guinea pig mother, 'before impregnating a female of the species.'

Her mother squawked loudly.

'And it can form a conga line, also known as a piggy train,' said Merridy. She had swept the matter of the missing baubles skilfully under the carpet, but such sweepings tend to re-emerge at inconvenient moments, such as now, and bite one on the proverbial bottom. Or in this case, Hazel's bottom, although fortunately for Hazel, his bottom was only being sniffed.

Merridy was now almost resigned to a plethora of miniature creams, variously endowed with prize-winning crests, authoritative ridges and abundant rumps. She looked out of the window. The piggy train of the minute had, as usual, the Angel Hazel at the front. He was the engine. He was leading the train this way and that at breakneck speed. Little Spot's front feet clutched Hazel's tiny derriere, and Choklit's front feet grasped Little Spot's larger one. Chestnut was the caboose. He made a well-endowed and sizable caboose. His front feet gripped onto Choklit's haunches.

The piggy-train had the aspect of a furry millipede, since sixteen twiddly legs were its propulsion.

Suddenly there was a derailment, as the engine did an about-face, and the carriages and caboose crashed into one another. 'Oh dear,' said Merridy.

Hazel regulated the bottom-sniffing problem by learning to nip. He became a swift and efficient nipper. His front teeth were razor-sharp, and beware the pig that sniffed Hazel's bottom for too long. Hazel could about-face in record time, and the sniffer pig would get a razor-sharp nose-nip.

Hazel became known as Hazel Pink-Ears Little Nipper Pugh.

'Galloping Galloways!' said Merridy as Hazel nipped Chestnut on the nostril.

Hazel sat in a corner, guarding his rear end. He sucked up a blade of grass and stared balefully at the other guinea pigs. Not even the Originals were a match for his swift nose-nips.

Then Hazel started to scratch.

He scratched his back.

He twisted round like a corkscrew and tried to scratch with his razor-sharp teeth.

He stretched into impossibly acrobatic positions and scratched with the sharp claws on his back feet.

Hazel was itchy.

'Perhaps it's from too many conga lines,' Merridy speculated, for Hazel's skin scraping had cultivated nothing, and so it could not be a skin fungus. Hazel glared at his mother with a get-me-weetbix glare and Merridy hopped to it. The itchy Hazel was nippish and cross.

It was spring, and a lot of other Hobartians were itchy, but few of them had been the engine to a conga line. The week of balmy spring had brought with it a lot of spring pollen, and everyone's eyes itched, and their noses itched, and they sneezed and snorted and snuffled.

'Perhaps you have hayfever,' said Merridy to Hazel, who was crossly ingesting his weetbix. It was hard to tell.

Then Hazel scratched a pink patch on his back. It was completely bald.

Merridy was horrified. 'Look!' she wailed to her mother, who had fortuitously arrived bearing dandelions and marzipan scrolls. She had come to collect the Originals and take them home to Alexander Scott.

They took Hazel to emergency. His immaculate golden pelt was ruffled from the conga line, and now it was further sullied by a bald patch. Merridy stroked his head in the waiting room, and smoothed his sides, and spoke in a soothing tone, hoping to cheer the miserable Angel out of his indignities. But Hazel shook his mother off irritably. The waiting room was bare and cold and had no grass, and Hazel was miffed.

The vet on duty was a young lady. The guinea pig mother and her mother watched as she examined Hazel on the stainless steel examining table.

'What a pretty guinea pig she is,' said the vet.

'He,' said Merridy firmly. 'Hazel is a boy.' Surely the vet should know.

'But Hazel is a girl's name,' said the vet. Merridy's eyes met her mother's, but they did not mention *Watership Down*. Nor did Merridy ask the vet to inspect Hazel for baubles. She was clinging to the last vestiges of hope.

The vet examined Hazel's pink bald patch.

'Nasty,' she said. 'This will need oinkment.'

Oinkment? thought Merridy, and looked at her mother, but her mother hadn't noticed. Perhaps she had misheard.

Hazel was peeved. His beautiful black eyes glowered and his pink lower lip pouted adorably. He twisted athletically like a professional contortionist and scratched his pink bald patch with a vengeance.

'We must stop him scratching,' said the vet, which was stating the obvious. Hazel glared.

'What about those collars,' suggested the guinea pig grandmother. 'The ones dogs wear to stop them scratching off their scabs.'

They looked at Hazel's neck. But a guinea pig neck isn't much of a neck. There is nothing for a collar to hold onto.

'Wait a minute,' said the vet. She went into another room. Merridy held Hazel gently on the stainless steel table, and stroked his golden fur. Hazel didn't squeak, because he was sick of being poked about on a stainless steel table.

The vet came back holding a pinkish article with holes at both ends. 'A tubular bandage,' she announced.

The vet inserted Hazel into the tubular bandage.

It was a mistake.

Hazel leapt onto the vet's chest. He bounced back onto the stainless steel table. He hurtled into the air and did three somersaults and a triple bypass. It was a terrifying sight, Hazel in a pink tubular bandage doing a triple bypass. Merridy grabbed the catapulting Hazel and clutched him to her throat. Hazel bit Merridy's nine-strand bead necklace and beads sprayed across the stainless steel table.

'He doesn't like the bandage,' observed the vet perspicaciously as the guinea pig grandmother tried to catch three hundred and sixteen tiny glass beads. 'He got a fright,' she stated, which was hardly a brilliant observation, thought Merridy. Hazel's tiny heart thumped like butterfly wings against her throat as she clutched him tightly. She had not bothered to try and catch the beads, in case of dropping Hazel and giving him a heart attack.

'We mustn't get him too stressed,' said the vet, whom Merridy was beginning to think was a complete dunderhead. The vet left the room for more equipment.

Hazel's eyes bulged. He wanted out.

Merridy and her mother ferried Hazel home in the black travel bag. The first guinea pig emergency had been expensive and traumatic, but at least Hazel could no longer scratch.

At the sight of their returned engine, Chestnut, Choklit and Little Spot stood up against the chickenwire of the playpen. Their front legs peddled and their noses sniffed frantically.

Merridy hoisted Hazel out of the travel bag with a flourish. 'Hazel has slippers!' she announced. Hazel glowered at his welcoming party.

The slippers were pinkish and matched Hazel's skin perfectly.

'Now he can't scratch,' explained the guinea pig grandmother.

The welcoming party's legs had stopped peddling.

The slippers were on Hazel's hind feet. They were makeshift slippers, made of pink elastoplast. They looked ridiculous.

Merridy popped Hazel into the playpen.

'And,' she said, 'we have oinkment!' Hazel glared. He crouched in the middle of the playpen like a small and belligerent bull in a Roman arena. He was ready to fight off all bullfighters, train carriages and sniffer pigs.

But no pig came forward. Choklit, Chestnut and Little Spot looked warily at the newly slippered and anointed Hazel. He looked and smelt funny. And they didn't want an oinkment-and-slipper-scented engine.

Then Hazel stamped his hind feet. He ran quickly in a circle.

He ran faster and faster, but he could not outrun his slippers. It was a ridiculous sight, the sight of a stamping, slippered guinea pig speeding about in a one-pig conga line.

The guinea pig grandmother squeaked a nose squeak of amusement, and Merridy snortled, because she wanted to give Hazel his dignity, and did not want to laugh a full-blown laugh.

Hazel stopped running. He was irked. He tried to scratch his back, and couldn't. He chewed a slipper in annoyance. He stamped a slippered foot and gnawed at the other. It was a bad end to a bad day, and the Angel Hazel was disgusted.

'We will soothe your itch with *oink*ment,' said Merridy in a squashed sort of voice, because she was holding in her snortles. 'Three times a day.'

'And you will be absolutely fine,' she said to Hazel Pink-Ears Little Nipper Pugh. 'Even if you *are* bottom pig.'

13

Another sort of bottom pig

Choklit and Little Spot's visit left the Cherub Chestnut positively assertive. For an anxious pig, his behaviour was remarkable. He stalked Hazel incessantly and leapt onto his back like a bareback rider whenever Hazel was distracted by eating. His passionate embraces were not well received, but Chestnut had become remarkably agile at avoiding sharp nose-nips. He had become accustomed to the slippers and oinkment, which no longer put him off.

'Chestnut Pink-Foot Little Humper Pugh,' said Merridy affectionately to her beloved mongrel. Hazel's position as reigning male had been short-lived, and Chestnut had taken over.

The altercations were constant. Chestnut Pink-Foot pursued Hazel Pink-Ears round and round the playpen, and the jumping and humping was followed by sharp nose-nipping and all-too-brief breathers in various pigloos. Hazel sometimes lay in wait outside Chestnut's door, to get in first with a nose-nip, and Chestnut's pigloo would move about like a headless turtle until he saw a suitable opportunity for pouncing. The perpetual drama was entertaining but exhausting. Fortunately for the guinea pig mother, at night times the altercating halted in favour of sleep. Merridy was pleased to see Chestnut developing confidence, but wished that his confidence had turned out less boarish.

One evening after dinner, Merridy noticed an anomaly. She was scraping the last of her tuna pasta with vine-ripened tomatoes and kalamata olives off her plate, because she liked a clean plate at the end of a meal, and she was watching the guinea pigs in their pink sparkly box. Chestnut was ignoring Hazel, who was tearing up strips of newspaper, and he had not even touched the tomato scraps. This was not normal behaviour for the newly assertive Chestnut. And it was not normal behaviour for the ordinary Chestnut either. He looked sluggish and miserable.

Merridy picked up Chestnut and placed him gently on the kitchen carpet, which was a treat, because it meant running. She put Hazel on the carpet next to Chestnut, as incentive. Under normal circumstances, which is to say, the new normal, Chestnut would have lunged towards Hazel's buttocks and pursued him under the kitchen table. But Chestnut didn't even glance in Hazel's direction. Hazel scampered off, popcorning gleefully. His new flourescent orange slippers flashed.

Chestnut did not move.

Merridy offered Chestnut a celery stick. Chestnut chewed a disconsolate chew and stopped. He waddled a little way along the kitchen carpet.

Holy macaroni! thought Merridy, trying not to squeal out loud and frighten the guinea pigs. Hazel watched furtively from behind a cushion. He was chewing on the orange slippers.

Chestnut dragged his bottom a bit further. He looked very uncomfortable.

Merridy lifted Chestnut off the kitchen carpet and peered

underneath him. Holy cows and saddleback hogs! she thought. What on earth is that!?

There was a knock at the kitchen door. Merridy rushed to open it, holding Chestnut upside down like a fat baby in her arms. 'Chestnut has a problem!' she gasped at Hector Protector. 'I think he's going to burst! I think he's eaten too much!' she said, 'Help! It's an emergency!'

Hector Protector came indoors. He was unperturbed, because he was excellent in a crisis. He pulled a bar of peppermint dark chocolate out of his jacket and put it on the kitchen bench for later. Merridy was distraught, and didn't even notice the chocolate. 'Chestnut can't walk properly,' she hiccupped. 'He's waddling as if he has a carrot up his fundament.'

Hector Protector, to his credit, kept a straight face. Chestnut did look overly swollen in the nether regions, which might feasibly be around the intestines, and his fundament looked uncomfortable, as if it were harbouring a substantial blockage.

'Let's google,' he suggested calmly, 'guinea pig constipation.' He reached for the Apple laptop. Chestnut lay in Merridy's arms looking wretched. Hazel skipped behind the couch and deposited an artistic arrangement of chocolate raisins. He was having a whale of a time, because nobody was humping him, or sniffing his bottom, and his mother had forgotten all about him.

Hector Protector put on his glasses and perused the Google offerings. He looked studious and reassuring. Hector Protector knew how to soothe cases of nerves, and looking studious and reassuring helped. 'Olive oil,' he read. 'It will lubricate the intestines and assist the passing of waste matter.' In other words, it would help Chestnut to expel the blockage and reduce his swelling.

Merridy held Chestnut in her arms while Hector Protector fed him olive oil with a teaspoon. It was Chestnut's first time being fed with a teaspoon, and he sucked in the olive oil like an expert. Merridy massaged Chestnut's tummy to help the olive oil.

Then Hector Protector broke open the peppermint dark chocolate. The guinea pig mother was cheered and hopeful, and the chocolate gave a kick to her endorphin levels, which felt superb.

Hazel, entirely overlooked, cavorted merrily in the bedroom, leaving small cairns of Hazel-presents in strategic positions. He left the remnants of an orange slipper under an armchair and stamped his bared foot with glee.

After a while, something began to happen. The olive oil was working. Chestnut produced a chocolate raisin so large it might have been mistaken for a prune. 'I have never been so glad,' exclaimed Merridy, 'to see a prune!' Chestnut produced a second raisin the size of a plump olive. After fifteen consecutive raisins he began to look more comfortable and detectably less swollen, and the raisins had assumed a normal size. 'Go Chestnut go!' cheered Hector Protector.

And Merridy, because she was a dedicated guinea pig mother, and because this is what mothers do when things become a little constipated, helped by squeezing Chestnut's bottom. 'It seems,' she said to Chestnut Pink-Foot, 'that you are another sort of bottom pig.'

'It was a great relief,' said Merridy to her mother and Alexander Scott, who were sharing a telephone receiver, 'because the pocket-pet vet is expensive, and emergency visits are exorbitant.'

'Prunes are very good for the bowels,' said the guinea pig grandmother, who ate prunes with her muesli on a daily basis.

Alexander Scott giggled. 'But he did not eat prunes,' he said, 'he had olive oil!'

'Yes,' said Merridy. 'And his blockage was the *size* of a prune, and then an olive, and then the normal-size chocolate raisins.'

She was nursing the unblocked Chestnut on her lap, who had regained his eating function and was tucking into a cauliflower floret.

'It was lucky he didn't have to have an operation!' said Alexander Scott, who thought a guinea pig bowel operation would be most interesting.

'It is indeed,' said Merridy, who could not imagine what a guinea pig operation would cost, and didn't want to.

'Is Hazel still bald?' asked Alexander Scott. 'Does he need a hair transplant?' He had been watching a hair transplant operation on television, and was entranced by the plantation effect. 'They plant the new hair in rows,' he said.

Merridy laughed. 'No transplant,' she said. 'He's grown his fur back, and I've stopped putting on the oinkment.' Hazel was lazing on remnants of striped sock, and a flourescent yellow thread was disappearing into his pink mouth. 'But I'm keeping him in slippers,' said Merridy, 'just in case.'

Hazel's slippers required constant vigilance, for he had become an expert slipper-remover. Merridy wondered where most of the slippers went, and suspected ingestion. She kept a range of slipper options to hand, which she rotated for variety and because she liked symmetry. The slipper options were more attractive than the vet's slippers, which had been made of pale pink elastoplast. Merridy wrapped on a blue pair, because Hazel had chewed the orange ones, and then the flourescent yellow ones, and then the parrotfish pink, which were bright enough to glow in the dark. Now it was time for a blue pair, and then it would be time for flourescent orange again. Hazel lay back on his mother's lap and watched her face as she wrapped on the blue slippers. He did not kick, because he knew he would shortly have the slippers off.

And for a while there was peace in Flat Three, for Hazel was distracted by his slippers, and Chestnut was simply relieved to be unblocked. 'My two bottom pigs,' said Merridy fondly, feeling rather pleased, because two bottom pigs were calmer than two top pigs, and she was happy to have a household sans reigning male.

14

A matter of breeding

'IT'S AMAZING,' SAID MERRIDY to the guinea pig grandmother on the telephone, 'that there are so many breeds of guinea pig!' She was flipping through her latest resource, which detailed the many breeds of guinea pig along with excellent illustrations. It was a hefty tome borrowed from the library. Behind the hefty tome, a pedigree cream and a handsome mongrel lay wedged together on her lap.

'There are English guinea pigs, and American guinea pigs, and Abyssinians, and Peruvians,' said the guinea pig mother as her listener said 'Ooh' and 'Aah' with interest. 'There are guinea pigs called Shelties and there are Angora guinea pigs.' She examined a picture of an Abyssinian guinea pig. It was tufted all over with spiky rosettes. It looked as if it had won the entire set of rosettes at the Hobart Guinea Pig Show.

'I thought guinea pigs all came from Peru,' said the guinea pig grandmother.

'Like Paddington, but without suitcases,' laughed Merridy.

'Maybe they did, once upon a time.' She looked at the guinea pig illustration of a designated Peruvian. It was staggeringly handsome with a mane of luxuriant hair. 'One day,' said Merridy, 'I would like a designated Peruvian.' She imagined a luxuriantly maned Peruvian with a small suitcase that said 'Wanted on Voyage'.

Suddenly Alexander Scott came on the telephone. 'What's a Peruvian?' he demanded.

'An inhabitant of Peru,' said Merridy, 'which is in South America. It must have a cold climate because Peruvian guinea pigs have long coats.'

'I want a Peruvian!' exclaimed Alexander Scott.

'The book says you need to cut their hair,' said Merridy, 'and wash it frequently.'

'Oooh nooo,' said Alexander Scott. 'That sounds like a lot of work.' He already had a lot of work tidying up two guinea pigs' chocolate raisins, and keeping their roosting box clean.

Merridy looked at the next picture. It was labelled 'Himalayan' but the guinea pig reminded her of a Siamese cat. It was white all over with dark ears and a dark nose. It was absolutely ravishing.

'One day,' she said to her nephew, 'I would also like a Himalayan.'

'Me too!' asserted Alexander Scott, picturing a snow-white guinea pig scaling Mount Everest with a pickaxe.

'I think,' said Merridy, 'that Chestnut is descended from an American Crested guinea pig crossed with a Dutch. The American Crested is Chestnut's colour with a white rosette, and the Dutch sort is patterned white and orange in Chestnut's pattern.'

'Phew!' whistled Alexander Scott, who was bent into a pretzel shape. He wriggled a lot while on the telephone.

'So Chestnut has pedigree in him after all,' said Merridy, 'although it's a bit mixed up.'

'Haha,' laughed the pretzel, who was wound through the back of a kitchen chair. 'Chestnut is a pedigree mongrel! Like Choklit and Little Spot.' It was true. Choklit and Little Spot were also mongrels, but with pedigree somewhere in their ancestry.

Merridy laughed. 'Hazel is our only pure pedigree,' she said, looking at her pristine cream boar with his immaculate blonde pelt and his beautiful black eyes. The pristine boar looked as if butter wouldn't melt in his mouth. His adorable chin rested comfortably on Chestnut's shoulders, and Chestnut's head rested comfortably under Hazel's tummy. It was the only bit of himself that would now fit underneath Hazel.

The guinea pig grandmother came back on the telephone, because her rambunctious grandson had bounced off to his trampoline. 'And in Peru,' she announced, 'they eat them!'

'I know,' said Merridy, who didn't want to, but had accidentally been confronted with pictures of guinea pigs schnitzeled and kebabed, and even roasted with tiny chillis in their mouths. Google did not discriminate between pleasant and traumatic images of guinea pigs, and presented the lot. She had imagined Chestnut roasted whole, and it had been a horrible thought, even if he would make a fine roast, whereas the Angel Hazel would not. A roasted Hazel would be a piteous roast, like roasted quail, delicate and bony and not worth the trouble.

Merridy would one day be mother to several more breeds of guinea pig, including a Peruvian-Abyssinian from the police force, but in the meantime she had her work cut out for her with one pedigree cream and a handsome mongrel.

Chestnut Pink-Foot and Hazel Pink-Ears had moved into a vacillating phase. They could not decide who was top pig and who was bottom pig. They switched from bottom to top and back again, sometimes several times a day.

'Perhaps this means,' said the guinea pig mother, 'that nobody is the reigning male. Or maybe they are both top pigs and this is going to go on for perpetuity. Or perhaps they are still both bottom pigs, because neither pig is able to dominate the other in a consistent fashion.'

A third possibility, which Merridy preferred to ignore, was that Hazel might be a bossy girl pig, and that Chestnut might be trying to impregnate her. For despite Hazel's increasing stature, he still had no balls, which continued to give the guinea pig mother anxious twitches. Occasionally her efforts to ignore the question were overridden by an urge for certainty, and she would consult her references yet again. But the diagrams were as useless as ever. 'If I followed these,' said Merridy to Hazel, 'you would be a girl.'

'But you are not yet pregnant, so you must be a boy.'

To add to the confusion, while Hazel was androgynous in looks, he was in behaviour, boarish. And whether his lack of apparatus was because he was a girl, or an immature specimen with internal and undescended bollocks, who could tell?

In the meantime, thought Merridy, I will keep acting on the assumption that he is a boy, and treat him accordingly.

'That's ridiculous,' she said, catching herself in the middle of the thought. 'Treat him accordingly?! What, give him toy cars instead of a barbie doll?' She contemplated Hazel, who looked heavenly in the pink sparkly box because the pink set off his pink rose-petal ears and immaculate golden pelt. 'The only reason,' she said sternly to the Boar Adorable, 'that it is important for you to have balls is so that we don't end up with guinea pig babies! Two babies is quite enough.'

The Boar Adorable looked demurely at his mother, and suddenly, without warning, threw his hindquarters at Chestnut, which was a very boarish manouvre.

Merridy flinched. The gender identity question was giving her a headache.

'I daresay I'm prejudiced in my expectations,' she said to Hector Protector, 'for I expect boars to *look* boarish *and* have boarish apparatus.' She rubbed her aching eyes. 'But at the same time, I want them to behave in an *un*boarish manner, because their boarish behaviour is difficult. Which is ridiculous, because boars should be able to look and behave like boars. Whatever a boar is, and whatever boarish behaviour is!' She sank her throbbing head down onto her arms, which rested on Hector Protector's capacious dining table. 'If a boar doesn't have boarish apparatus,' she said, her voice muffled, 'is he still a boar…?' Her voice trailed off, because her brain powers had been exceeded.

'I think,' said Hector Protector kindly, 'that you are stuck in the dual gender dichotomy, which does not allow for variation.'

Merridy said nothing. Her brain hurt.

'The dual model is inadequate,' explained Hector Protector carefully, 'because it divides everyone into two sorts, to help us simplify and understand differences. But sometimes someone is born with mixed apparatus, or none at all. And even someone who looks like a boy may not behave like a boy.'

'I know,' groaned Merridy. 'I'm fixated on the issue of apparatus. Because if Hazel is a boar and behaves like boar, and looks like a girl, and even behaves like a girl, it doesn't matter. As long as he is a boar!'

'But how do I tell he is a boar if he has no balls?!' The guinea pig mother was agitated. If Hazel was a girl pig behaving like a boar, this was a problem. But if Hazel was a boar without balls, then she was safe.

'Well,' said Hector Protector comfortingly, 'he is not pregnant yet!'

And so far as the guinea pig mother could see, this was true. For the one definite outcome at this stage of the proceedings, which is to say, six months after the Hobart Guinea Pig Show, was that Hazel had produced nothing beyond several thousand chocolate raisins. Nor was he obviously pregnant. Hazel's delicate hindquarters were becoming almost robust, but his waist remained taut and slim.

Hazel now weighed in at seven hundred and twenty grams. 'That means you have doubled in size,' said Merridy, 'since arriving at Green Street.'

Chestnut, at nine months, still won out when it came to robustness. He had been born six weeks sooner, and had the further advantage of an unstoppable eating function. Unless it was stopped by constipation, thought Merridy, but that had been a one-off, and Chestnut had launched back into unstoppable eating as soon as he had been unstopped. Chestnut's waist was almost as wide as he was broad in the beam. And if Chestnut's waist was wide and unpregnant, it was highly unlikely that Hazel's slim one was.

'I think you have also doubled in size,' said Merridy, who could not be sure, for Chestnut had shot the needle past its one kilogram limit.

15

A timely manifestation

CHRISTMAS WAS RAPIDLY APPROACHING. It was hard to remember a time before she had been a guinea pig mother, thought Merridy. She remembered the Hobart Guinea Pig Show, and the rows of guinea pancakes on their flying carpets. She remembered finding the tiny blonde angel-pig splayed on top of his bed of hay for all the world to see. And she recalled searching for a little friend for him, and finding the Mongrel Chestnut with his handsome crest.

It was hard to remember a time when there was no playpen on the Green Street lawn, and no pink sparkly box in the kitchen for a guinea pig bed, and no need to buy extra weetbix and guinea pig muesli and bags of hay. Or a time when the rustle of guinea pigs was not heard in the middle of the night, and the sounds of newspaper shredding.

And there had been a time before she had worries about guinea pig apparatus, or skin fungus, or how to cut *piggus* toenails without snipping the quick. She had not known about top pigs and bottom pigs and the *piggus* pecking order. She had not known about boarish behaviours and she had never seen a guinea pig conga line. She had certainly never imagined a guinea pig needing slippers.

The world of *guinea piggus domesticus* was endlessly intriguing, and it had been a most instructive year.

'An excellent thing about year ends,' said Merridy to the *piggus* Hazel and the *piggus* Chestnut, 'is Christmas.'

'Unless,' she added, 'you have a great deal of late Christmas shopping to be done. In which case, Christmas is a nightmare and should be banned.'

The Cherub Chestnut looked confused. The Angel Hazel looked bored. Merridy thought they looked ravishing. She imagined the Cherub Chestnut wearing a Christmas hat, and pictured the Angel Hazel in a tinsel halo. Merridy had never cared for cherubs before Chestnut. But Chestnut made an irresistible cherub, with his white crown and his adorable pink lips.

It was Hazel and Chestnut's very first Christmas.

Merridy showed them how to decorate a Christmas tree. She had silver tinsel which was soft and fine. It had been used for decades of Christmas trees. And she had tiny ornaments.

'When I was a little girl in Africa,' Merridy said to Hazel and Chestnut, 'the Christmas trees were juniper. They had a lovely juniper scent. But this is a miniature spruce,' she said, trailing tinsel around its summit. 'I like my Christmas tree potted,' explained the guinea pig mother to her students, 'because it is clean and green and can be reused.' The miniature spruce was potted in a bright blue pot.

Hazel tested a silvery speck of fallen tinsel. It was more slippery and less pleasing than shredded newspaper.

Soon the potted spruce was a silvery pyramid glistening with tiny ornaments. There were tiny red stockings, sewn by Merridy when she was young. There were tiny golden bells on red and green ribbons. There were miniature clay figures threaded onto fine cotton. There were shiny stars. And there was a glass angel on top. The angel didn't look at all like the Angel Hazel.

Underneath the tree Merridy put her ancient nativity scene. There was Mary, and Joseph, and the baby in the manger. There were shepherds, and three kings with cloaks and crowns and presents. There was an angel blowing a trumpet. This angel didn't look at all like the Angel Hazel either. Hazel didn't have a trumpet.

Hazel looked grumpily at the nativity scene. It did not smell appetising. Hazel did not eat small clay objects, however beautifully crafted by his mother.

Merridy noticed that something was missing. The nativity scene was from a previous era, and there were no guinea pigs.

The next morning Merridy packed the fishmobile. The Angel Hazel was being particularly demanding, with bring-me-grass looks and give-me-another-politician stares. He had also perfected a new expression. It was a tickle-me-at-once expression and very effective. Hazel looked at his mother with his tickle-me-at-once expression and if she obeyed, rewarded her with musical squeaks of appreciation.

Merridy packed her antique cardboard Mr Bean suitcase in the boot. The Mr Bean suitcase was battered with a corner missing, but it was still an excellent suitcase. Today it was full of presents.

On the floor in front of the passenger seat she put the black travel bag, with fresh shredded newspaper for her boys. Hazel tried another tickle-me-at-once expression. Merridy was busy but for some reason she could not resist Hazel's new trick. She sat down at once and picked him up and stroked him on her lap. Hazel closed his eyes and rewarded his mother with a short musical symphony.

In the north of island, the ancestral household was in a furore. Alexander Scott lay on his stomach with his head poked into a confetti bush. The guinea pig grandmother scurried round the rockery wielding a spatula. To escape the pandemonium, Young Grandpa had retreated to the back garden to weed in peace.

Choklit and Little Spot had escaped.

They were slippery pigs, and difficult to catch.

The Christmas turkey was ready for the oven, and being severely delayed.

The guinea pig grandmother was in a panic. Little Spot was in the middle of the rockery, somewhere. But each time she caught sight of him, he dived under another bush. The rockery was too big, and Little Spot was too slippery, and the spatula was too short.

Alexander Scott was lying in wait. Choklit sat stubbornly under the confetti bush. It was a deep confetti bush and Alexander's arms were not long enough to reach Choklit. So he lay in wait.

Choklit and Little Spot were behaving very badly. It was their second Christmas. 'You won't get any presents!' scolded Alexander Scott.

'I must put the turkey in the oven!' flapped the guinea pig grandmother, and rushed off.

At Green Street, Merridy finally put down the Angel Hazel to finish packing. It was a delightful sort of day, with the mountain almost cheerful under a blue sky. Forget-me-nots scattered the green lawn. She gathered a sheaf of fresh dandelion stems and laid this into the black travel bag. Chestnut stuck his head out of the newspaper.

'*Padkos!*' said Merridy. 'That means food-for-the-road,' she instructed. 'In Afrikaans. It's an important South African tradition, boys, and very useful during long car trips!'

Chestnut dragged a dandelion stalk under the newspaper. He would be hiding for two hours and forty-five minutes, which was how long it took Merridy to drive the fishmobile from Green Street to the ancestral household in the beautiful Tamar Valley. There would be a fifteen-minute break at Campbelltown, by the river, for grass, when Chestnut would take his head out to eat.

At the ancestral household, the turkey was finally in the oven. The guinea pig grandmother fanned herself in relief.

Outside, Alexander Scott had come up with a plan. It involved a broomstick.

Alexander Scott poked the broomstick into the confetti bush. Choklit watched the broomstick warily. Alexander Scott aimed the broomstick carefully at Choklit's bottom. 'Gotcha!' he said, and Choklit shot out from underneath the confetti bush. Alexander lunged athletically towards the bolting Choklit and tackled him to the ground. Choklit dug his stumpy legs into the lawn and pushed. But Alexander had a firm grip around Choklit's middle. 'Gotcha!' he yelled, and scooped him up. 'Naughty boy!' he said. Choklit enjoyed being in Alexander Scott's embrace and forgot about escaping. He squeaked deep chocolate squeaks. He was fat and round and looked like a Guinea Buddha.

Alexander popped the Guinea Buddha Choklit into the now very secure guinea pig guest accommodation. He resumed operations, poking the broomstick carefully into the rockery to see where Little Spot was hiding. Little Spot shifted to a clump of carnations. He was a slippery pig.

'Gotcha!' puffed Alexander Scott, as the broomstick prodded Little Spot's rump. Little Spot made a dash for a pocket of nasturtiums, but the broomstick was relentless. Little Spot raced onto the lawn. Alexander Scott performed another athletic lunge. Trampolining paid off when it came to this sort of thing. Little Spot shrieked in protest as Alexander's grip closed around his hips. He wriggled and kicked. Alexander turned Little Spot upside down. 'Naughty pig!' he said, looking into Little Spot's upside down eyes. 'You won't get any presents!'

Sometime later the fishmobile zoomed into the driveway. It was a tranquil scene. Young Grandpa was weeding the rockery. Choklit and Little Spot nibbled weeded-out dandelions. And Old Grandpa was carrying a bucket of non-edible weeds to the compost bin behind the house. Merridy opened the fishmobile door and breathed in the scent of warm grass.

Then the guinea pig grandmother emerged. She looked a bit hot under the collar. 'The guinea pigs escaped!' she cried. She was still feeling an excess of cortisol after the chase. Alexander Scott burst out of the front door, wearing a red Christmas stocking on his head. 'But I caught them!' he bellowed. 'Wheek wheek!'

Merridy lifted the black travel bag out of the fishmobile and Hazel tried his tickle-me-at-once expression on his grandmother. 'Gosh!' said the guinea pig grandmother. 'She is much longer!'

Merridy's eyes popped. 'He!' she said, as the guinea pig grandmother picked up the Christmas Angel and cuddled him to her chest.

Young Grandpa came indoors after a while. 'There's something funny going on with those pigs,' he said. 'A lot of bottom-sniffing.'

'Oh dear,' said Merridy, who was unpacking her Mr Bean suitcase. 'It's a conga line.' She had expected a conga line, because Little Spot and Choklit had been reunited with their engine, who was once again pristine and slipperless.

Alexander Scott and the guinea pig grandmother rushed outside to spectate. Merridy said to Young Grandpa, 'It's all Hazel-bottom-sniffing, I suppose.'

But then, as they stepped onto the front verandah, something happened.

Hazel, the angelic and speedy engine, applied the brakes. The conga line was flung over its twiddly legs, crashed noisily into a pigloo and ran squealing up the ramp and into the guest bedroom.

Hazel Pink-Ears had had enough. He had dug in his pink heels and thrown the bottom-sniffers off.

Alexander Scott crowed with excitement, because Hazel was chattering his teeth, which meant a pigfight was in the offing. The guinea pig grandmother held her breath, because Hazel was puffed up like a tiny lion and mercilessly nipping the heels of the conga line as it disappeared upstairs. Old Grandpa appeared carrying a pair of clippers and said, 'She's a feisty little chap!'

Merridy said nothing. Hazel was on the rampage, and she hoped it would not involve blood.

But Hazel stopped at the bottom of the ramp. He chattered his teeth up at the bedroom doorway, out of which peered three anxious faces. It sounded like rattling sabres. The upstairs pigs seemed thoroughly cowed, and Merridy could have sworn that they looked guilty, but surely guinea pigs did not have a moral sensibility, and so how could they look guilty, even if they ought to.

Hazel settled at the bottom of the ramp. He ate a grassblade thoughtfully, and sucked up a white lawn daisy with casual elegance. He munched on a dandelion stalk, and chewed the yellow flower petals with delicate precision. His beautiful black eyes were slanted under their long eyelashes, and he looked innocent, and pure, and unruffled. And determined to keep his lawn all to himself.

Alexander Scott sighed. 'No pigfight,' he lamented.

'No pigfight,' repeated the guinea pig mother with relief.

It seemed that Hazel had thrown off his status as bottom pig.

Christmas Eve dinner was a big dinner in the ancestral household.

'When I was a little girl in Africa,' said Merridy to the guinea pigs as they lolled about the guest hutch lawn, 'it was too hot to cook on Christmas Day. So we had a Christmas Eve dinner, and on Christmas Day we ate leftovers. That's why we're having a big dinner tonight.'

Hazel was in excellent spirits. He had received a gold tinsel halo, and chewed it into three pieces. He had chased Little Spot and Choklit round the guest hutch lawn until they cowered in a corner, and banished Chestnut to the upstairs bedroom. Hazel was being top pig, and he felt like a king, even if he was still the smallest.

Merridy was resting briefly after a brisk spell in the kitchen. Two spectacular Christmas trifles now filled up the ancestral fridge, and the turkey filled up the ancestral oven.

Alexander Scott had insisted on making an Alexander sort of trifle, while Merridy made the usual trifle. Alexander's trifle had large jelly blobs in it, and an unusual arrangement of Swiss roll on the bottom. It also had a great deal of custard. Merridy's trifle was a more balanced affair, with a neat Swiss roll mosaic. There were fresh raspberries and a lot of glacé cherries in both trifles. Alexander had added several large fifty cent coins to his, pre-washed, which were likely to break a few teeth.

Alexander and Merridy covered their trifles with white whipped cream. There were fresh cherries from the beautiful Tamar Valley to decorate the top. Alexander planted a grove of mint-leaf Christmas trees in his snowy trifle landscape. Merridy cleverly made sliced kiwifruit into a Christmas tree shape on top of hers. The cherries went around the edges. They were huge plump dark cherries, with stalks on.

'Silver balls!' cried Alexander, and threw silver balls energetically and randomly into his mint-leaf forest.

Merridy neatly dotted her silver balls on the ends of her kiwi-tree branches.

The top pig Hazel puffed up his silky golden pelt like a cloak and lazed in the middle of his lawn, looking for all the world as if he deserved a crown.

Christmas Eve dinner commenced with the arrival of Alexander Scott's mother, who had only just finished her Christmas shopping. 'Mum!' hollered Alexander, 'I helped make the trifles!' His mother placed a pile of colourful parcels below the Christmas tree, with a tramp-champ gymnastically wrapped about her left thigh. 'One for the guinea pigs,' she said, pointing to a cheerful red number as the sound of an electric carving knife started up in the kitchen. 'They've been very naughty!' giggled the tramp-champ. 'They don't deserve a present!'

Christmas Eve dinner was a roaring success. The Christmas ham and turkey were magnificent. The roast potatoes were roasted to perfection. The peas and beans and carrots were delicious with the turkey gravy. There were no brussels sprouts.

'Jingle pigs! Jingle pigs!' sang Alexander Scott. He was extremely full, and wearing a lop-sided sparkly bonnet. 'Wrestle me!' he cried, but nobody wanted to wrestle, for Alexander's uncle, who was a ruthless and willing wrestler, was brushing up his *muay thai* in Bangkok at that particular moment, and everyone else was too full to move. 'I wish my uncle was here,' complained Alexander Scott, who missed him dearly when he was off on worldly travels.

Merridy went outside to fetch some distraction, and her bonnet fell off. She returned bearing guinea pigs. It was quite an armful. Little Spot, Choklit, Chestnut and Hazel all looked at the Christmas table. Their necks lolled over Merridy's arms, and their legs lolled underneath. Four guinea pig bottoms were rudely displayed, but the guinea pig mother could not carry four guinea pigs at once without displaying their bottoms.

'Look!' squealed Alexander Scott, pointing at the guinea pigs' nether regions.

Everyone looked.

'Hazel Pink-Ears has turned into a boy!'

And it was true. Hazel Pink-Ears had finally grown male apparatus.

And so the second year of the Guinea Pig Era was drawn to a fitting close. That night, as Merridy lay like an overfed dugong in her bed, she mused on the evening's doings. The Angel Hazel had finally sprouted balls. This was an excellent development. With his halo and his balls, Hazel was surely destined to be king pig. Her little golden angel. Hazel Baby. Her once teeny-tiny fairy cream. Hazel was an up-and-coming boar with attitude, and now, finally, he had the balls to fit.

Merridy rolled onto her side, feeling like a beached whale. This was the proof everyone had been waiting for. It proved that Hazel would never be impregnated, not even by a conga line of boars. And there would never be thousands of Hazel-replicas eating her out of house and home, thought Merridy dozily, and that was a great relief. One Hazel was quite enough.

The twentieth day

MERRIDY WAS WRUNG OUT. Each morning for twenty days she had woken with a colossal headache, as if something massive had landed on it in the night. A heffalump, perhaps, or a mastodon, or possibly something bigger, like Argentinosaurus, the heaviest known dinosaur in the history of planet Earth.

Each morning when she opened her eyes, just a crack, to see what kind of day it was, she saw the Pig God watching her from above the meditation shrine, his lucid gaze compelling. He looked self-assured and smug. He was much bigger than the Buddha on the meditation shrine.

'Resistance is futile,' uttered Merridy weakly. 'It's my fault, for hanging your photograph in prime position in the bedroom.' She felt shackled by two solid gold guinea-pig sized shackles, one on each leg.

The Pig God seemed to have grown in the last twenty days. Was his ego being inflated by the stream of Hazel-centred literature being churned out, day after day? thought Merridy. Could an overfed ego weigh as much as Argentinosaurus?

Merridy grunted as her brain banged about inside her throbbing skull. She wasn't sure how much more she could take.

After a shower and breakfast, Merridy sat down gloomily at her Apple laptop. It was time for her daily penance. She could feel the pressure building. Each day as she showered and breakfasted and saw to the guinea pigs, it built to a crescendo inside her head and wanted out. And the only way to out it was to type. The nuisance was that outing it relieved the pressure only temporarily, until the next morning, and then, there it was again. 'Out!' she said. 'Out, out!'

The first-ever guinea pig novel was manifesting at speed. Its author had just manifested the Pig God's long-awaited baubles and was feeling intensely relieved. 'I'm on the home stretch now,' she said to the small ginger guinea pig watching her from beneath his ginger crown. He was cleverly concealed behind a paint can on the kitchen floor, but Merridy could still see one intelligent dark eye. Jupiter was playing spying games with his mother.

Fortunately Merridy did not realise she had made a significant miscalculation. The home stretch would make scaling Mount Kilimanjaro look like a walk in the park. It would take many months, a truckload of chocolate, and another nine hundred pages.

Hazel One-Eye's good eye floated leftwards across the Apple laptop screen, filling it with a stare of magnified reproach. There seemed to be a bug in the screensaver, because it was stuck on the Royal Portrait and Merridy was unable to change it. She quickly logged onto Facebook, which was one way of getting rid of the reproachful eye. The Pig God Hazel disappeared briefly, but reappeared on Merridy's profile page where he perched on her green fluffy dressing gown looking fat and glossy and inert.

There was no escape.

'This is very difficult,' said Merridy reprovingly. 'I'm an editor, not a novelist, and you are making me write a novel!'

Hazel continued to look solid, smug, and supreme. In fact, with an ego density now equal to twenty solid gold Argentinosauruses, he was immovable. Not even Guy Fawkes with all his explosives would shift the beast.

Part Two

The Wounded Emperor

1

An April Fool

IT HAD BEEN A GLORIOUS SUMMER. The mountain had put on an uncharacteristic display of good temperament, and the days had been long and sunny and warm and blue. Merridy had been in her element, because there was nothing she loved so much as warm sunny summer weather. The Angel Hazel and the Cherub Chestnut had eaten themselves into a stupor on the burgeoning summer weeds, until the dearth of rain had shrivelled the Green Street lawns into a crisp and dusty arena better suited to rodeo displays than genteel grazing. Then they took it in turns, kicking up the dust with their little feet as they pursued one another round the chickenwire-covered playpen. It was an amusing sight, the sight of Chestnut riding Hazel bareback around the playpen, and the sight of Hazel throwing him off and leaping onto his abundant rump like a small and furry cowboy. The guinea pig rodeo made Merridy laugh as she watered the thirsty pot plants. It was most entertaining being guinea pig mother to a pair of boars, both of whom wanted to be reigning male.

Chestnut's confidence had increased along with his girth, and he had become a solid and dependable pig. His favourite activity was still eating. He ate for enjoyment, and for pure delight, and for research purposes (when his mother tossed in a different sort of vegetable, for instance), and for comfort when a comfort-needing situation arose.

Hazel's girth had also increased, and with the long-awaited manifestation of his male apparatus had come a growing sense of entitlement. Now that he had some, he was throwing his weight about, and his beautiful black eyes often held a belligerent look under their long eyelashes. But his build retained its elements of delicacy. His tiny feet were still delectably pink and sweet, his rose-petal ears were still paper-thin and perfect, and his pink lower lip still pouted its irresistible little pout. He was still the Angel Hazel to the guinea pig mother, who was as besotted as ever, and he was still the Impeccable Cream to the Mongrel Chestnut, whose fur got ruffled during rodeo displays, whereas Hazel's did not.

The guinea pig mother could always rely on the dependable Chestnut for a welcoming wheek or a cuddlesome squeak, but on the capricious Hazel, she could not. Hazel sometimes turned his back on his mother and sulked, and sometimes he gave her get-me-grass looks, which in a time of drought was wilful and unfair, and sometimes he lay in her arms like a furry baby, rewarding her with musical symphonies of approval. It was much easier being mother to the Mongrel Chestnut, and Merridy wondered if Hazel's moodiness was due to his breeding, which of course it was, or due to his personality, which of course it was too.

And then the Green Street residence was thrown into disarray.

It was April Fool's Day, which in Tasmania is officially one month into autumn, but Tasmanian seasonal beginnings are impossible to predict, and in Hobart one is just as likely to be presented with a wintery snowfall on April Fool's Day as a graceful shower of deciduous leaves. Today the mountain had decided on a heatwave and so the guinea pig mother was in shorts.

'I can't believe you've been at Green Street for almost a whole year,' Merridy observed to Hazel and Chestnut at breakfast. The front door was wide open to let in the scent of morning, and she was eating a bowl of human muesli with milk. Hazel was chewing his weetbix in a contemplative fashion, and Chestnut had finished his and was looking hungrily but warily at Hazel's. There was no guinea pig muesli this morning, because the guinea pig mother had run out.

Then the telephone rang.

Merridy was expecting a telephone call from the guinea pig grandmother, who always tried to trick her on April Fool's Day even though she was usually too astute to be tricked. 'Squeak!' squeaked Merridy, which was what she answered when she knew it was the guinea pig grandmother, but not other persons telephoning, because they did not understand guinea pig language.

'Squeak!' replied the guinea pig grandmother. 'I told Alexander Scott that Hazel was pregnant with thirteen babies!' she announced breathlessly.

'But Hazel can't get pregnant!' objected Merridy, who thought it was an odd choice of trick since Hazel had manifested visible balls on Christmas Eve, settling the question of his gender once and for all.

'April Fool!' snorted the guinea pig grandmother. She was in fine fettle, and feeling mischievous.

Merridy laughed. Of course her mother would not have tried such an obvious and inaccurate trick. She was more devious than that!

'Actually,' said the guinea pig grandmother, 'your sister is pregnant!'

Merridy wasn't falling for another pregnancy trick, and laughed again.

But it was true. The mother of Alexander Scott was expecting, and this threw the Green Street residence into disarray.

'I'm going to be a brother!' announced Alexander Scott, hopping from one leg to the other in excitement. 'And I have always, always wanted a baby brother or sister!'

'You'll be the best brother in the world!' said Merridy warmly.

'Yes!' said Alexander Scott. His chest was puffed up with pride, but Merridy could not see it because she was two hundred and seven kilometres further south. Then Alexander's chest deflated, and Merridy heard it because it sent a rush of air into the telephone receiver. 'But,' he sounded suddenly uncertain, 'I don't think I can be the best brother in the world and a guinea pig father at the same time.' He gripped the telephone tightly, and a tear squeezed out of his left eye. Merridy could not see the tear, but she could hear it in his voice.

'I'm eight years old now,' he explained to Merridy sadly, 'and I'm at school all day, and at trampolining all afternoon, and Choklit and Little Spot are lonely without me.' He sniffed, and the tear trickled down his left cheek. 'And when my baby brother or sister is born…' His voice faltered.

'It's all right,' said Merridy kindly, for her heart ached to hear her nephew tearful and sad. 'I will look after Choklit and Little Spot for you. Your mother is getting ready for your baby brother or sister, which is exciting, but will be tiring. And she'll need your help. Your guinea pigs can come and live at Green Street.'

'Ohhhh, thank you!' said Alexander Scott fervently. He wanted to laugh and cry at the same time, because he was going to be a brother, and he longed to meet his baby brother or sister with a great longing, but he would miss Choklit and Little Spot with a great missing. He would miss their wheeks and rumbles, and he would miss watching them in their chicken coop when he practised trampoline. But Alexander Scott was an expert guinea pig father, and he knew Choklit and Little Spot needed lots of attention to be happy. He hiccupped, and choked back a sob.

'It's my pleasure,' said Merridy, and she meant it, for Choklit and Little Spot were the next-best guinea pigs in the known universe to Hazel and Chestnut, and looking after four boars would surely be twice as much fun as looking after two. 'They will be very happy with Hazel and Chestnut, and you can come and visit!' she said to her nephew to cheer him up. 'We're only two hundred and seven kilometres away, and that's not very far at all!'

Alexander Scott suddenly felt light and happy. He saw himself visiting his hippy aunty in her colourful eyrie, and being greeted hysterically by Choklit and Little Spot, who were fat and content and shiny and ecstatic to see their father again.

Merridy suddenly felt cold all over. She saw Choklit and Little Spot escaped from their low-slung chicken coop, languishing thinly among the thorny rose bushes, orphans in their own home, and nobody noticing because they were busy feeding a new fat human baby.

She shivered. The thought of an orphaned guinea pig was tragic, and the thought of the orphaned Originals was more tragic still. 'One day,' she said to her nephew suddenly, 'I will have a guinea pig orphanage.' And she saw the Green Street back lawns edged with guinea pig hutches housing dozens of rescued guinea pigs. A large sign above the back fence read in cheerful red lettering: *Pig Heaven – The Green Street Guinea Pig Orphanage*. All of a sudden she felt elated, and a surge of energy flooded her body with warmth.

'Yes,' she said to Alexander Scott, 'and it will be called Pig Heaven!'

And so the Ridgeback Little Spot and the Guinea Buddha Choklit came to live at Green Street, in Flat Three. They came to live in the chickenwire-covered playpen with the Angel Hazel and the Cherub Chestnut, because Alexander Scott was going to become a brother, and no one wanted them becoming orphans in their own home. They were the first rescued guinea pigs to come to Merridy's eyrie.

And so Merridy became mother to a boar quartet.

2

The Green Street quartet

THE ARRIVAL OF THE ORIGINALS plunged the Green Street residence into a state of pandemonium. Logic and arithmetic dictated that two more boars should double necessary care and maintenance, since two is half of four, but something exponential was happening which bypassed simple calculations and boggled the guinea pig mother's brain. A quartet seemed to demand ten times the management of a pair of boars. It was exhausting, and required specialist skills, which the guinea pig mother was developing at speed.

This was not to say that the Guinea Buddha Choklit and the Ridgeback Little Spot were difficult pigs. Choklit was placid and gentle and minded his own business, and Little Spot, when he was not playing a screaming damsel, was no more rambunctious than any other pig.

It had to do with guinea pig dynamics. Because whereas before, only Hazel could bother Chestnut, or Chestnut could bother Hazel, now Hazel could bother three pigs, and so could

Chestnut, and sometimes Hazel would bother two pigs together, and sometimes all three. And when Merridy applied her mathematical nous to the problem, it seemed that where two boars yielded two sorts of possible botherings, four boars yielded a possible twenty-four. Which explained why it felt like ten times the amount of work, because in fact, it was twenty-four.

And so Merridy had her work cut out for Year Three of the Guinea Pig Era. For not only had Hazel manifested a timely Christmas gift along with his growing ego, but she had four boar pigs on her hands.

The guinea pig mother was watching the four boar pigs on the Green Street lawn. It was good to be able to say with complete assurance, 'four boar pigs', thought Merridy, watching Hazel leap onto Chestnut's appetising rump. Hazel was flaunting his new baubles as usual, and Chestnut escaped into a pigloo. He was turning into a recluse, because Hazel kept chasing him, and then lying in wait outside the pigloo, and Chestnut would not come out.

Little Spot grazed peaceably on the pseudo-marsupial lawn, with one eye out in case the flaunting baubles came too close. Hazel shifted his focus to another target, and leapt towards Choklit, who was placidly minding his own business. He chased Choklit round the pigloos until he hunched in a corner, weeping. This jerked Merridy to attention. It was a heartrending sound, the sound of Choklit weeping. He looked thoroughly cowed. Merridy lifted the lid off the playpen and hoisted the Guinea Buddha into her arms. 'Poor Choklit!' she crooned, and Choklit shoved his nose deep into her armpit. His tummy felt gloriously stout to Merridy's caress. Merridy sat on the rickety swing seat and rocked him gently back and forth.

'Hazel!' she said sternly. 'You are being a bully!' Hazel slipped carelessly into a pigloo, with his baubles sticking out of the doorway. Hazel had ways and means of showing his opinions, and this was one of them.

It was hard to tell who was reigning male in the new regime. 'It comes down to a contest,' said Merridy to the guinea pig grandmother, 'between Hazel and Little Spot. Because Choklit is a placid pig and minds his own business, and Chestnut is becoming a recluse.' Chestnut's burst of confidence was being diluted by extra-long periods in solitary confinement. 'Perhaps there can be two top pigs?'

'Oh dear!' said the guinea pig grandmother anxiously, because she was thinking of Choklit weeping in a corner with a bitten bottom, and Chestnut pinned perpetually into a pigloo by Hazel. 'What will you do?'

'I think,' said Merridy, 'that we need larger accommodation.' Possibly twenty-four times larger, she thought. As she spoke, the top pig Little Spot threw his bottom meanly at Choklit, which was a very boarish manouvre, shoving Choklit away from the carrot he was placidly chewing. Choklit and Little Spot were in their lime-green sleeping box with its pleasant underlay of shredded politicians, but it was not suited to bottom-throwing manouvres, because the recipient of the thrown bottom had nowhere to go. The Guinea Buddha looked mournful and hungry, and Little Spot sat on the stolen carrot, because he had already eaten and didn't want another one, but he didn't want Choklit having one either. 'A plastic box is only big enough for a two-pig bed if the two pigs are getting on,' concluded Merridy. She glanced into the pink sparkly container, noting that Chestnut was being a recluse under the sports pages, and that Hazel was being top pig on top. He whittled like a beaver at Chestnut's carrot, which was available because Chestnut wasn't coming out.

'But what about the playpen?' queried the guinea pig grandmother, because the playpen was a lot bigger.

'Even the playpen with four pigloos for privacy is not big enough,' said Merridy, 'because it is not in proportion to the dynamics of a boar quartet.'

And so Merridy went in search of proportional accommodation.

The local pet shop sported a fine selection of hamster wheels and colourful cages for other, less appealing rodents. But these were useless for guinea pigs. They were too small, and besides, guinea pigs are not allowed hamster wheels because it gives them backache.

Merridy addressed the shop attendant. 'Guinea pigs,' she said. 'I want suitable accommodation for four boars. One pedigree and three mongrels. They are behaving badly and need larger quarters.' The shop attendant looked alarmed, and directed Merridy to an expansive pet emporium further down the Channel Highway.

The pet emporium boasted an impressive display of guinea pig housing. There were bottle-green pens with wheels. There were dove-grey hutches with chickenwire and double bedrooms. There were wooden triangular pens like large bars of Toblerone chocolate. There were square pens and hutches with ramps and guinea kennels with Gothic-style doorways.

But there was nothing bigger than the chickenwire-covered playpen. Perhaps, thought Merridy, other people's boars are docile and need less personal space. She looked at a row of dog kennels. The doorways were much too big for guinea pigs.

Then Merridy saw it. It was at the back of the emporium, between a pair of semi-circular aluminium chicken coops. It was a guinea pig palace.

'Ohhhh!' said Merridy, the air in her lungs rushing out in one long pleasurable sigh.

The guinea pig palace was perfect. It was enormous. It was made of warm red cedar, with two storeys and a peaked green roof. It had a ramp from the ground floor to the top floor, and on the top floor was a verandah with a view, and a separate master bedroom. The doors fastened with little wooden love-heart fasteners. And there was even a secret hatch, to catch guinea pigs by surprise. 'I need that hatch!' said Merridy.

The guinea pig palace was too big to fit in the fishmobile, so Hector Protector brought his capacious ute. It took both of them to heft the guinea pig palace into the back of the ute, and both to heft it off at Green Street.

They planted the guinea pig palace strategically in the middle of the Green Street lawn. 'It looks magnificent!' said Hector Protector, rubbing his palms together. Hazel eyed the palace with suspicion from the doorway of his pigloo. 'And I will be able to monitor boarish behaviour from the kitchen window,' said Merridy, subsiding onto the rickety swing seat. With increased grazing space, a ramp for exercise, a verandah and a master bedroom, there was more than enough space for four boar pigs, and she expected their behaviour to be excellent. But there was the secret hatch, just in case.

The guinea pigs adapted quickly to the guinea pig palace. They did not miss the chickenwire-covered playpen in the slightest. Even the Angel Hazel discarded his reservations in favour of the upstairs verandah, which offered a suitable viewing point for top pigs.

Merridy taught the guinea pigs to use the ramp. They were intelligent pigs and caught on fast. Then they scurried up and down with alacrity, and sometimes too quickly, which meant an undignified tumble.

Merridy tested the secret hatch. She opened it quietly and quickly and caught Little Spot by surprise. Little Spot put on his distressed-damsel expression, and screamed with his mouth wide open and his back teeth showing. 'Drama-pig!' said Merridy, tickling the drama-pig under his chin.

The guinea pig palace was fantastic. It was in perfect proportion to the dynamics of a quartet of boars. Chestnut could be seen grazing outside his pigloo while Hazel lazed on the upstairs verandah in the sunshine. Little Spot took over the master bedroom in the daytimes when he felt like it, and guarded the doorway. Choklit minded his own business in tranquillity.

And because it was still warm, and because of the spacious master bedroom, Merridy let the guinea pigs sleep outdoors at night. She filled the master bedroom with hay, and the guinea pigs cuddled together for comfort and warmth. It was a heart-warming sight, the sight of four snuggling guinea pigs in their hay. But Merridy missed their company indoors. At dusk she said goodnight to her four boar pigs, looking into the master bedroom to see them snuggling together. 'I miss you!' she would say. 'I miss you being in the house at night with me. But I'm happy you like your master bedroom!'

At night time, while the guinea pigs snoozed snugly in their hay, the guinea pig mother dreamed a new dream. She lay in her pink bed under the window, the stars sparkling above, and sometimes the full moon flooded the room with its silver light. And when she drifted into sleep the dreaming began.

Sometimes the sign had green lettering, and sometimes blue, and once it was obscured by flowering clematis. The back fence of the garden was always bathed in sunlight, which warmed the hutches of the rescued guinea pigs. The rows of hutches were sometimes wooden with upstairs bedrooms, and sometimes they were like a row of tiny boatsheds painted blue, white, yellow and red. Sometimes the garden was walled with red brick, and sometimes sweet peas twined up its trellising, shedding their fragrance on the gentle breeze. Sometimes strings of colourful prayer flags fluttered in the branches of the overhanging alder, and the guinea pigs played in drifts of yellow autumn leaves. Once Alexander Scott was in the garden, feeding sweetcorn to a glossy black guinea pig with shining eyes; and once Old Grandpa was there, raking up the leaves and putting them into the compost bin beneath the alder tree.

And always the dream was warm, and golden, and safe.

This was Pig Heaven.

3

A serious omission

MEANWHILE, EARTHLY EVENTS and her earthly flock kept Merridy busy, for the Green Street quartet attracted a cohort of regular but select visitors. Hector Protector regularly brought vegetation from his garden, and Merridy's girlfriends regularly brought their small children. The guinea pig mother restricted visits to mornings so that she had time for other activities. 'Otherwise,' she said to Hector Protector, who was an exception and could visit whenever he felt like it, 'I can't keep up with my editing.' She remembered the copious streams of visitors when Hazel and Chestnut had arrived at Green Street. It had been absolutely exhausting. 'Or the housework,' she added.

Hector Protector nodded approval. He was cosseting Hazel Pink-Ears, whose pink ears looked transparent in the morning sunlight, and whose beautiful black eyes were closed.

'Several of my girlfriends now have children,' noted Merridy as she prepared a morning tea of sliced pink lady apple, celery sticks and chocolate biscuits. The celery sticks and pink lady slices were for smaller visitors to offer the guinea pigs, and the chocolate biscuits were for the humans. Sometimes the two got mixed up.

'Green Street offers an important communal service,' Merridy pronounced, 'because we offer guinea pig feeding and cuddling, which is a genteel outdoor activity and much better for human children than tv.'

Merridy only offered communal services under close supervision, to keep the guinea pigs from being poked or squashed. Small human visitors needed instruction, and she was happy to provide it.

'Hazel is always the favourite,' said his mother. Hazel opened his eyes bashfully beneath his long lashes, which was an act because he was not bashful in the slightest. He was pleased to offer communal services because it meant being fed and pampered by several large humans and numerous small ones. He enjoyed being force-fed celery sticks, and was happy to be mauled about.

'Mummy's tummy is growing!' announced Alexander Scott, who was still rather puffed from a vigorous workout on his trampoline. 'And I must be careful not to squeeze it!'

His hippy aunty was squeezing the Royal Cream, who was definitely not expecting – besides expecting an excess of attention, that is. Hazel was in a mood for being squeezed, and squeezed a *piggus* melody into the telephone.

'Is that Hazel?' asked Alexander Scott.

'It is,' affirmed Merridy.

'I can tell,' said Alexander, 'because Chestnut sounds like a squeaky door, but Hazel sounds like musical instrument!' He giggled. Alexander was an expert on musical instruments because he played the flute in an orchestra. 'And Choklit has a deep rumbly voice, and Little Spot is a drama-pig.'

'Yes,' said Merridy, who sometimes played four instruments in a *piggus* orchestra.

'I've been thinking about my guinea pig orphanage,' said Merridy to her nephew, who was the reason she had guinea pigs in the first place, and four boars instead of two.

'You can have every kind of guinea pig!' said the culprit with gusto. 'And when my baby sister or brother is grown up, I can come and help you!'

Then Alexander Scott thought of the vast piles of chocolate raisins that would need to be swept up, and said quickly, 'Unless I become a pocket-pet vet. Then you can bring all the orphans to me for operations!' He felt excited at the thought of hundreds of guinea pig operations.

'I hope,' said Merridy, 'that the orphans will not need too many operations.'

'Oh but they will!' said Alexander Scott, who was confident that he could operate on any number of orphans.

'None of our guinea pigs have had operations,' noted the guinea pig mother, which was jumping the gun.

'Oh but they will!' said Alexander Scott eagerly, also jumping the gun, but in his case, somewhat more accurately.

Merridy had assessed the whereabouts and wherewithals of Tasmanian guinea pig orphanages, of which there was a frightful deficiency. 'I cannot locate a single guinea pig orphanage south of Bass Strait,' she announced to her mother, 'which is a terrible omission!'

The guinea pig grandmother huffed with indignation.

'Did you know,' continued Merridy, 'that some people think guinea pigs are just for children?'

'Really?' The guinea pig grandmother sounded surprised.

'And would you believe,' added Merridy, 'that some people treat guinea pigs as *disposable pets*.'

The guinea pig grandmother drew in her breath, for this was a shocking revelation. 'What is a *disposable pet*?' she asked incredulously.

'One that you *throw away*,' said Merridy. Her mother was speechless. 'I know. It's a travesty.'

'But they are intelligent creatures and need proper care!' said the guinea pig grandmother.

'Yes,' said Merridy. 'But it seems they are brushed off as cute but lacking in brains and personality. And because people think they only live as long as hamsters, they think they needn't bother, and thousands of guinea pigs die each year from neglect, and thousands more are dumped, because people get sick of them.' She had been reading about guinea pig rescue on Google, and the truth was scandalous and tragic.

'It's an unspeakable disgrace,' insisted the guinea pig grandmother, which it was.

And Merridy looked at Hazel and Chestnut, whose personalities required a good deal of proper care. She could not imagine how anyone could see a guinea pig as a disposable pet.

'There ought to be an education program,' insisted the guinea pig grandmother, who was a firm believer in education.

'And pet shops should be banned from selling guinea pigs,' asserted Merridy, who was mounting a favourite hobbyhorse.

'And there should be laws against the keeping of only guinea pigs!' said the guinea pig grandmother, who felt sorry for only children, and therefore for only guinea pigs.

'Yes!' said Merridy. 'An only pig is a lonely pig!'

There was a pause in the conversation, during which Merridy and her mother pictured thousands of lonely only pigs all around Tasmania, needing a rescuer and a busy guinea pig orphanage where they could be social and happy.

'Switzerland already has a law against only pigs,' said Merridy, for her research had thrown up surprising information.

'And in Canada, you may not keep guinea pigs outdoors unless they have heated accommodation!'

It was comforting to think of such laws, and there was another pause in the conversation as Merridy and her mother contemplated the thought of heated guinea pig accommodation, which would be excellent in the Tasmanian winter.

'I suppose it's because they are not wildlife, to be rescued by wildlife rescuers,' said Merridy, returning to the topic of orphanages. She pulled the telephone line away from Chestnut's jaws, because his incessant eating didn't stop at telephone lines, which made old-fashioned telephones a health hazard. 'And perhaps because they are smallish and easily overlooked.' But not Chestnut, she thought, whose bottom is enormous and makes him difficult to overlook.

'But there are Dog Rescues and Cat Centres and Raptor Refuges and Devil Parks!' protested the guinea pig grandmother, who was an expert on animal rescue. She had rescued several wallabies in Cataract Gorge already, and had once rescued a wombat in the garage.

It was true. There were rescues for canines and felines and raptors and reptiles and even an aged equine rescue and a rescue for goats. Which was a considerable lot of rescues for a small island. But there was not a single guinea pig rescue, refuge or orphanage.

That must mean a lot of orphans, thought Merridy. 'I googled it,' she said, 'and the nearest guinea pig rescue operation is one hundred kilometres south of the Queensland border.' And she wondered how many lost guinea pigs wandered the cold streets and dismal bushland of Tasmania, seeking warmth and company. It was a horrid vision, and she determined to set her sights on establishing the island's first-ever guinea pig orphanage.

'I will need a different landlord,' she said, for while the landlord was amenable to a small flock, he might object to a large influx of orphans. 'Or a lot of money,' she added, imagining offering the landlord a fine sum for the entire Green Street premises, and turning them into Pig Heaven.

'I suppose the RSPCA takes guinea pigs,' speculated the guinea pig grandmother.

'They do,' said Merridy, 'but they're in with large fierce creatures like Doberman Pinschers, which do *not* suit orphaned guinea pigs.'

4

Guinea pig design and function

MERRIDY WAS AT THE DOGGY BEACH. It was at the end of Green Street, the beach end of course, and there hordes of hounds, mongrels and pedigrees pranced and strutted and chased one another or the seagulls up and down the shore. None of them were orphans, for they all had owners with leads and balls and sticks and other doggy equipment. The dog owners rushed about after their dogs or gathered in small groups to discuss doggy politics and compare canine attributes.

Today was a crowded day for the Doggy Beach, and Merridy was feeling left out. She wanted to bring her boys to the beach for walks too, but on less crowded days to be safe from the attentions of Alsatians and Doberman Pinschers. Merridy watched a particularly adorable sausage dog trotting through the grasses with its tail held high. Merridy had fancied a sausage dog until she met Choklit and Little Spot. After that she had fancied guinea pigs more than anything.

She observed the Shitzus and Labradoodles and Chihuahuas.

Surely a Chihuahua harness would fit a guinea pig, she thought. The Chihuahuas in question boasted spring-green harnesses with tiny golden studs. Those Chihuahuas would look quite appealing in their harnesses, thought Merridy, who liked spring green, if they didn't look starved and rattish. She imagined the guinea pigs, who were wholesome and rounded, trotting to heel in an organised and docile conga line. They are much better-looking, she thought, which was a shallow and unworthy thought but nonetheless, in the guinea pig mother's opinion, true.

Not long after, Merridy was in the pet emporium looking for a new sipper bottle to replace one that had sprung a leak. The shop attendant saw Merridy stop dead in her tracks and utter the words, 'Brilliant! Absolutely brilliant!' Then he saw her jump three small but distinct jumps. It was odd behaviour for a customer.

Merridy had taken on the habit of popcorning when excited, and had forgotten she was in a public place where adult humans did not usually jump about. The sight of a row of harnesses had attracted her attention. They were harnesses with long leads for guinea pig walking. There was no mistake, because each was labelled 'Guinea Pig Harness', next to a picture of a harnessed guinea pig.

'Brilliant!' she said again. 'Absolutely brilliant!' She had also forgotten about the sipper bottle.

'I will buy four,' she said. 'Two red, and two blue.' There were no spring-green ones with golden studs, but red would complement Hazel's blonde tresses and Choklit's brunette fur, and blue would look entrancing with Little Spot's orange ridge and Chestnut's stylish rosette.

Merridy absent-mindedly handed the shop attendant a loyalty card for wood-fired pizza, being in a blissful daze of imagining herself parading up and down the Doggy Beach, with onlookers going 'oooh!' and 'aaah!' and 'never seen such a sight!' and the local newspaper arriving to photograph her orderly flock. She would become famous as the Guinea Pig Queen of Green Street, for her pigs would be the only pigs in Hobart to wear designer harnesses, and it would set a trend, and guinea pig walking would become the in thing.

'Could I have your credit card?' said the shop attendant warily.

Merridy was thrilled. Back home, she offered Choklit his new crimson apparel. Choklit looked askance. He nibbled at some grass. She called out to Hazel. 'Hazel! Look at your new harness! You will make a noble steed!' Hazel looked unconvinced. He was already noble, thank you very much.

Merridy took matters into her own hands. She lifted Choklit and settled him on her lap. He was the ideal combination of intelligence and zen calm, and most likely to take to his harness at once.

There were a lot of small silver buckles and red straps and Choklit's feet got in the way, but finally Merridy said 'Now you can roam like a free pig!' which was a contradiction in terms, since the free pig was tethered by a lead to his mother, but pride clouded Merridy's logic.

Merridy placed Choklit on the ground and stood, stretching the lead out to test it for length. Choklit sat inert, like a plump chocolate pudding.

'Come on, my boy!' said his mother encouragingly. And the tethered pig Choklit made an experimental lunge. He squealed as the lead jerked him onto his back. It was most undignified, and Choklit rolled wildly to regain his small feet, upon which he careered toward the falling-down shed with Merridy in hot pursuit. They raced up and down the lawn and round the guinea pig palace, as Merridy dared not stop for fear of accidentally strangling Choklit with the lead. Choklit halted suddenly in a corner, and bucked. Merridy beheld his rodeo performance with shock. 'Oh,' she whimpered, 'what have I done?'

Then suddenly there was peace.

Choklit had escaped his harness. Quivering, he swallowed a therapeutic dose of grass. Merridy's heart was going like the clappers. Perhaps Choklit isn't the right temperament for a designer harness, she thought.

The afternoon passed in a more relaxed but enormously frustrating fashion. Pig after pig escaped the harnessing. There was less bucking, since Merridy picked enclosed areas of indoor carpeting for training purposes. But the harnesses had a design flaw. The designer had clearly never seen a guinea pig.

Hazel slipped effortlessly once again from his scarlet rigging, thereby demonstrating the Hazel-Houdini Effect and illuminating the guinea pig harness design flaw. No matter how tightly Merridy strapped him in, he slipped out like a slippery eel. Hazel watched her boldly, waiting for the next strap-in so that he could slip-out.

'The problem is,' Merridy said to Chestnut, who was demolishing a spinach leaf beneath the couch, 'that guinea pigs have no necks. There is nothing to hold the harness.'

She hoisted Chestnut onto her lap, with his spinach.

'And,' she went on, 'guinea pig legs are short and slip out of the harness on the bottom side.' She wiggled Chestnut's front pink feet. They were fearsomely cute, with transparent pink toenails.

'But,' she concluded, 'the design flaws are not in fact with the guinea pig, which is a perfect design. They are with the harness, which ought to be designed for a round, neckless rodent with short legs, and not for a Chihuahua.'

'Guinea pigs are the perfect design,' said Merridy to her mother, having described how not to walk a guinea pig, 'and they function perfectly in accordance.' She watched Choklit twisting his torso to collect a personal pellet, which was a perfect example.

'Oh yes!' said the guinea pig grandmother, who still favoured canines and wallabies, but was an enthusiastic guinea pig supporter. 'Their shape matches their nature. They are funny and round, and cuddly and affectionate,' she said, 'and very intelligent.' Merridy's mother had studied psychology in her youth, and the nature of intelligence, so she could tell. 'And they recycle politicians into composting matter!' she said as an afterthought, which was an excellent example of good function.

'And they are wonderful company, and calming,' said Merridy, 'except when on a lead. Because a guinea pig is not designed for a lead.'

'And they eat weeds and banana skins and pumpkin peels, which saves on wastage,' said the guinea pig grandmother, who was off on an environmental tangent.

'I'm glad they're vegetarian,' said Merridy, who was squeamish about meat.

She looked at Hazel, who was the most perfect guinea pig design of all. His glossy flanks were still silky and soft, and gleamed in the lamplight. His languid eyes slanted ravishingly beneath his long lashes, and his little pink mouth pouted like a film star's.

'Also,' said the guinea pig grandmother, 'they save on lawn-mowing!'

'And,' giggled Alexander Scott, who had joined the conversation, 'they clean up their own chocolate raisins!'

'Which is why,' said Merridy, holding the Impeccable Cream on her lap, 'it's so hard to believe people don't understand their proper care.'

'They are a lot of work,' said Alexander fervently, remembering cleaning up the chicken coop and its roosting box. 'But I still miss them,' he said, for he missed having an audience for trampolining practice in the back garden.

'Well,' said Merridy as she stroked Hazel between his perfect pink ears. 'We may not be able to go to the Doggy Beach, but one day you will freely roam Pig Heaven.' It will be fenced in, she thought, the whole of the back garden, so the guinea pigs can be free pigs, and that will make poorly designed harnesses redundant.

5

Hazel scores again

MERRIDY HAD DISCOVERED that guinea pigs make excellent hot water bottles, which was a useful attribute if you lived in Tasmania. Merridy watched episodes of *Grand Designs* with at least one guinea hottie on her lap. Sometimes she cooked soup with a guinea hottie in each pocket of her fluffy green dressing gown. The guinea hotties were large and heavy and weighed down the fluffy green dressing gown, but they were warm. The guinea hotties squeaked sleepily as Merridy moved back and forth by the stove.

It was the first of June, and the Green Street quartet now slept indoors in the kitchen, for the nights were chilly. Summer was officially over, and midwinter on the horizon, and the mountain was behaving badly, which is to say, throwing out rainstorms and miserable winds across the reaches of the River Derwent and the Hobartian townships gathered along its shores.

To the guinea pig mother's delight, a substantial iris-papered contraption had appeared at the bottom of the fire escape one morning. She suspected a generous well-wisher, but there were no identifying marks.

The contraption made perfect indoor sleeping quarters for four boars, and the pink and green plastic boxes were retired in favour of this more generous sleeping arrangement. The guinea pigs took to the new sleeping arrangement at once.

The iris-papered contraption was large and rectangular, with a ventilated and removable lid which could double as a coffee table in the event of human visitors. Inside were two rooms with a connecting doorway, and the bedroom featured a slot into which a litter tray could be inserted from without. A litter tray filled with newspaper shredding made a cosy guinea pig bed. The whole edifice was papered inside and out with delicate blue irises, which fitted perfectly with the eyrie's blue and yellow kitchen. This pleased Merridy greatly, for she liked her décor orderly and colour-matched.

But the best feature of the iris-papered contraption was a perspex window the length of the larger room, which meant that with the lid on Merridy could still watch the guinea pigs, and they could still watch her. 'Guinea pig tv,' she said to the guinea pig grandmother on the telephone as she watched her boys through their perspex tv screen. 'It's better than *Home and Away*.' The program of the minute had the pedigree Hazel hogging the muesli, while the mongrel contingent paced gloomily at a safe distance.

It was time for breakfast. Merridy could hear a chewing sound as she approached the iris-papered contraption. She lifted off the lid. 'Good morning, boys!' she said cheerfully, noticing Chestnut working away diligently at the internal décor. 'You're messing up your wallpaper,' she said to Chestnut, who was absorbed in pulling away its edges with his teeth. 'And I'm not sure that it's good for the digestion,' she added. Although if the guinea pigs could digest local politicians, she thought, they could probably digest anything. Choklit poked his little chin in the air anxiously, for he was waiting for his weetbix, and was anxious that somepig might steal it first. But Merridy always gave each boar a weetbix, to be fair, although it took the boars some time to sort out whose was whose.

After breakfast, on days like this one, she let the guinea pigs out on the striped carpet for exercise. The guinea pigs were playful and energetic. They played the chasing-under-towels game, which amused her, as their round cuddly shapes looked funny tunnelling beneath the old towels she laid over the striped carpet. Then there was the find-the-oats game, with a special ball supplied by the guinea pig grandmother for intelligence training. Merridy hid oats inside the ball, and the guinea pigs rolled it around to make the oats come out of a small hole.

And there was the run-into-the-hallway game, which was strictly forbidden, because while Merridy thought extra wear on the striped carpet could only hasten the arrival of new, more pleasant flooring, the hallway was carpeted in fresher material and needed protection. But as soon as the guinea pig mother turned her back, eight pairs of stumpy legs scuttled toward the hallway and galloped onto its non-striped carpet, which was dowdy and therefore excellent for camouflaging chocolate raisins.

Today was no exception, for indoor confinement made the boys mischievous. A suspicious silence caused Merridy to raise her eyes from a less-than-fascinating thesis and exclaim, 'Boys! Not in the hallway!' She put down the Apple laptop. Four pairs of eyes gleamed from a dark corner behind the camphorwood chest. 'No!' she said, chasing the unruly quartet back into the kitchen and checking for camouflaged deposits. 'Stay in the kitchen, boys,' she ordered, 'or I'll put you back in your contraption.' Then she barricaded the hallway with cushions, a small table, and the retired pink sparkly box.

The Angel Hazel invented his own games to train his mother, although his mother thought she was training the Angel Hazel. His favourite was chasey-chasey. When he'd had enough chasing he allowed his mother to catch him, and rewarded her with a special post-chasing musical composition.

'I've taught Hazel to play chases!' announced Merridy excitedly but erroneously to Alexander Scott, who had telephoned for guinea pig updates. 'I chase him round and round the iris-papered contraption, and he's becoming quite fast and hard to catch!' Hazel lay comfortably on his side watching Merridy through the perspex tv screen.

'What program is on?' asked Alexander Scott, for guinea pig tv featured numerous programs depending on boarish moods and inclinations.

'*Get-away*,' said Merridy, 'because Chestnut, Choklit and Little Spot have gone into the bedroom to get away from Hazel, and Hazel is relaxing like a sunbather on the beach because he has got away from everyone else.'

'Haha,' laughed Alexander Scott. 'Hazel is top pig!'

Then Hazel discovered the litter-tray insertion gap, and squeezed through it. Merridy found him one morning lazing smugly on the outside of the perspex tv screen, with three reproachful watchers on the inside. No other pig could squeeze through the insertion gap, and Hazel did it night after night, for he still had the slimmest haunches.

Merridy called on the skills of Hector Protector to block the gap. 'I blame the harnesses,' she said, 'for teaching Hazel to slip-out.'

'Hazel-Houdini strikes again,' laughed Hector Protector as he nailed a narrow piece of wood expertly across the gap.

'And now I'll have to take the litter tray out from on top,' observed Merridy, 'which is *not* convenient.'

Hazel-Houdini looked at the large bearded visitor and turned his back. He enjoyed thwarting his mother, and would find other ways to do so.

And so Hazel invented the coming-up-to-bed game, which gave the guinea pig mother as much exercise as a yoga class. It required squeezing, stretching, bending and grasping, along with the occasional surprise snatch. For while the guinea pig palace was still proving a fine outdoors habitat for a boar quartet, it had thrown up a design flaw of which Hazel took full advantage. Its size made guinea pig catching difficult unless one had the arms of a gorilla, and Merridy did not.

At dinner time Merridy trotted down the fire escape with a green bag, upon which any free-roaming pigs pounded upstairs into their master bedroom and huddled in the far corner. Any lagging-behind pigs received a sharp nip on the haunches from Hazel-Houdini. And when Merridy twisted the love-heart door-fastener to their bedroom, Hazel-Houdini led the gallop onto the verandah and down the ramp. The guinea pigs squeezed against the back of their grazing area, and waited for their mother to insert her torso through the lower doorway to increase her reach. When she was halfway in, Hazel led the stampede, and the guinea pigs pounded up the ramp with glee and hid again in the master bedroom. It was most entertaining watching their mother squeeze into the downstairs level, and then out again. 'At least it keeps me flexible,' said Merridy cheerfully. She tried a special coaxing voice to persuade the guinea pigs up to dinner, but to no avail.

'It's time to use the secret hatch!' Merridy announced, brushing mud off her knees. Winter made the operation dampish and it was messing up her jeans. She walked around the back of the palace to the secret hatch. This was the last-but-one stage of the coming-up-to-bed game. She opened it quickly and grabbed

Little Spot, who shrieked like a maiden with a knife to her throat. Merridy stuffed him into the waiting green bag. Then she snatched Chestnut, which was easy, for his bottom was easy to snatch. 'Gotcha!' she said, and stuffed him into the green bag. She collared Choklit, who subsided with deep chocolate grunts into the green bag, which was becoming rather full.

Hazel still lurked in the master bedroom, for this was the best and last part of the game, with no other boar distraction. Merridy bribed him with a dandelion stalk. 'Come on sweetheart, my Hazel-Angel!' she coaxed, waving it about. Hazel stared at his mother rudely and ignored the bribe. He was a sweetheart when he felt like it.

Merridy was freezing. The green bag heaved and squeaked. Merridy gave up. 'I'll fetch you later,' she said to Hazel, and lifted the green bag over her shoulder.

Hazel decided it was game over, check mate to himself. He slipped out of the master bedroom and sat innocently on the verandah, waiting for his mother to pick him up. Merridy did so quickly, before the Hazel-Angel changed his mind and wanted a rematch.

6

There's no *piggus* like a snow *piggus*

RAIN BUCKETED ONTO THE GREEN STREET HOUSE and filled the gutters to overflowing. The rain cascaded in a thundering waterfall onto the laundry roof beneath Merridy's bedroom. The mountain was invisible because it was night time.

Merridy tossed fretfully in her sleep. She was visiting Africa in her dream, and was lost in a huge garden. It was the garden of the house where she grew up, but had expanded into a maze of meadows punctuated with thorny acacias. As she toiled up a grassy bank, she recognised the syringa tree where she used to hide with a pair of binoculars. The syringa was in blue flower, waving its flowery branches in the hot breeze. She crested the bank, and was pleased to see several sheep-sized guinea pigs grazing near the side of her old house. They were enormous, with huge round haunches and woolly fur, but Merridy could tell they were descended from Hazel, because the fur was distinctly and exquisitely blonde. A rush of happiness flooded her being like sunshine in summer. Then she leapt forward in alarm. The enormous sheep-pigs had begun eating a thorny acacia, and there was a strange roaring noise. The roaring noise was coming from inside her head.

Merridy woke up. The roaring noise was still inside her head.

'Oh my guinea pig aunt!' she groaned, wondering what she had eaten the night before and whether it had given her a kind of brain indigestion. The roaring was very loud. Perhaps it was the effect of too much ice cream.

Merridy sat up suddenly. 'It's a flood! The rivulet is flooding!' she squeaked. She could hear the water rising higher and higher up to the eyrie. Her brain indigestion took a turn for the worse. She peered out of the window above her pink bed. She couldn't see any flooding in the driveway, which was a relief, but the roaring continued. Galloping Galloways! she thought. It's a tsunami! She could hear it, a middle-of-the-night invisible tsunami, roaring up the River Derwent, about to break upon the esplanade and rush up Green Street sweeping away everything in its path. 'The guinea pigs!' gasped Merridy, seeing herself running up the road in her pyjamas with two guinea pigs under each arm. 'Help!'

Merridy hurriedly donned her fluffy green dressing gown and scuttled to the front door. She was afraid to open it in case the tsunami came rushing inside, but took a big breath and opened it very quickly. The roaring noise tripled in intensity. At once Merridy felt wobbly with relief. It was the broken guttering spouting a thundering waterfall onto the laundry's tin roof.

Next morning, Merridy woke to the sounds of copious dripping. It had stopped raining. The guinea pigs dozed undisturbed.

Merridy peered out of the window above her pink bed. 'Oh bollocks!' she said. The mountain was covered thickly with snow. 'Goodbye summer!' she grumbled. This was a superfluous thing to say, because she had said goodbye to summer on several previous occasions.

There was a distinct icy tinge to the air inside Flat Three. But being used to Antarctic weather events, Merridy was well-prepared. She threw on her fluffy green dressing gown and ugg boots, and stomped into the kitchen to uncover the guinea pigs for breakfast. 'Today,' she said, as Choklit thrust up his chin, questing for weetbix, 'you have special visitors. If,' she added, 'the road isn't snowbound, and they can get through.'

The visitors arrived on schedule, having negotiated snow hazards skilfully and with the aid of an appetising selection of *padkos*. '*Biltong!*' shouted Alexander Scott as he plunged through the front doorway. 'We saved you some!' He waved a packet at his hippy aunty, who said, '*Baie dankie!*' which is Afrikaans for 'thank you', for *biltong* was a South African delicacy and hard to come by. She shut the door quickly to keep out the Antarctic blast. Alexander and her mother seemed positively energised by the freezing conditions, which Merridy found astonishing, for snowy weather made her browse for plane tickets to the tropics.

'We brought confetti bush for the guinea pigs,' said the guinea pig grandmother, who sported an array of Tasmanian winter garb including thermals, a waterproof gortex jacket, gloves, and a bright red beanie. She rushed over to the iris-papered contraption where Alexander Scott was tickling somepig with a piece of *biltong*.

'They are vegetarian!' exclaimed the guinea pig grandmother. The tickled pig sidled off into a corner after sniffing the *biltong* with distaste. 'Gosh!' she said. 'Hazel is enormous!'

It was true, all things being relative. Hazel's beam was still less broad than Chestnut's, and his nose was still the most dainty boar nose, but compared to his former self, he was enormous, and still growing.

'I think he is now *top* top pig,' said Merridy. Hazel demonstrated his position by pecking his minions into order. Choklit,

Chestnut and Little Spot scuttled into the tv room so that Hazel could have the confetti bush all to himself.

'I'm not sure if I'd rather have a baby brother or baby sister,' said Alexander Scott later. They had eaten pumpkin soup, which was hot and nourishing, followed by Zoo biscuits, which in Tasmania were another rare South African treat. There was a strange non-African animal on the new era of Zoo biscuits, which could have been a guinea pig.

'A baby brother would like what I like,' said Alexander with logic. He tickled the guinea hottie Choklit who was warming his lap. 'But a baby brother might want to use my toys.' He saw his favourite toys being gummed and gnawed by a teething toddler. 'So maybe a baby sister would be best.'

Merridy stroked the guinea hottie Chestnut, who was cosily nested inside her polartec top. Chestnut felt as relaxed as a baby in the womb.

'I'm sure either a baby brother or sister will love you,' she said to Alexander. 'They'll be very happy to have a tramp-champ for an older brother.'

'Yes!' said Alexander, swapping his hottie. Little Spot screeched in protest, just as there was another screech from the window where the guinea pig grandmother was standing doing the washing up.

It was snowing.

Flurries of white flakes whisked across the Green Street lawn.

'It's snowing!' crowed Alexander Scott, discarding his guinea hottie rather suddenly.

'It's snowing!' echoed Merridy, who was excited despite herself.

'Mount Nelson!' cried the guinea pig grandmother. 'I want to go up Mount Nelson!'

The humans girded themselves for action. Even Merridy

could resist her violent aversion to the cold with real snowflakes whisking about her own garden. She pulled on an extra-thick beanie. 'Boys!' she said, 'we're going out into the snow!' She donned two pairs of gloves and an extra-large coat. 'Hazel!' she commanded, 'I need a guinea hottie!'

Hazel looked peeved, for he liked to issue commands, not obey them. But Merridy inserted him into a spare beanie, and into the arms of his grandmother, who cooed soppily. Hazel settled himself down and closed his eyes.

Mount Nelson was really only a hill. But it had spectacular views across the River Derwent. It was only five minutes from Green Street, and Merridy revved the fishmobile upwards. If it was snowing in the Green Street garden, at sea level, it would be blizzarding on Mount Nelson, three hundred and fifty metres up. Hazel dozed like a mammoth grub inside his beanie. He was in his element: individual attention, personal sleeping bag, constant fondling. Hazel twitched ecstatically in his sleep.

The snow on Mount Nelson was sparkly and deep. As they struggled out of the fishmobile Merridy's nose froze instantly in the Antarctic gale. 'I need a balaclava,' she said, which is what she had said every winter since arriving in Hobart, which was about twenty. 'And I need the guinea hottie.' She took the guinea hottie from his grandmother and stuffed him inside her pocket. He was a tight squeeze, but Merridy needed a guinea hottie to stop her freezing solid all over. Hazel squeaked and went to sleep again, like a fat blonde baby in a papoose. He was almost beyond being a pocket pet, unless it was a very big pocket.

Then the guinea pig grandmother threw a snowball at Alexander Scott.

'There's no *piggus* like a snow *piggus*,' said Merridy later as they stood beside three snow sculptures. They were flushed and breathless, except for Hazel who was still performing his hottie function inside a tight pocket.

Merridy photographed the snow sculptures next to her mother's boots. Her mother photographed Merridy with the snow sculptures against the magnificent view. Alexander Scott capered about catching snow with his open mouth. 'That one looks like Hazel!' he pointed, and it was true. The largest snow sculpture had delicate ears but a belligerent air. 'I made it,' said Alexander gleefully. 'It has balls!' Two large icy baubles protruded from the tail end of the Hazel-sculpture.

Merridy excavated the real Hazel briefly for a photograph with his *alter piggo*. Hazel's eyes narrowed at the sight of the snow pig with large protruding baubles. He did not get out of his papoose.

The snow pigs were the first-ever snow pigs to perch on a Hobartian car bonnet. They had perfect round haunches and pristine white fur and small pebbly eyes. The largest sculpture, to the left, sported a noticeable back end.

'It's a Hobartian tradition,' said Merridy to her nephew, 'to build snow things on your car bonnet when it snows.' The snow pigs wobbled as she reversed and then drove carefully downhill.

'And then,' said the guinea pig grandmother, 'you drive all the way down the mountain and see if they stay on!'

'We're only driving down a hill,' said Alexander, 'so they'll definitely stay on!'

Hazel dreamed pleasantly in his papoose, and could hear the screams of adulation as admirers flocked around his beanie. He did not see his *alter piggo* became a one-eyed snow pig as a pebble lost its mooring and sailed into a hedge. He did not know it was Alexander Scott screaming 'Wheee!' and 'Ooooh!' as the Hazel-sculpture lost a second eye, and then its head, and finally, on the last corner, shot off into a gutter.

The only bits left stuck to the car bonnet were two icy baubles.

But two whole snow pigs survived the downhill ride to Green Street, and were carried up the fire escape into the relative warmth of Flat Three. The real pigs sniffed the snow pigs, and decided they were not good eating. And so the real pigs returned to their real food and the snow pigs went into the freezer. Hazel was emptied out of his sleeping bag and nipped Chestnut out of pique, and Choklit out of irk, and Little Spot just because. Then he lay comfortably by the tv screen with his baubles pointedly on display.

Merridy made hot chocolate with marshmallows, and sat with her mother and two guinea hotties on the couch. They watched the snow clouds racing across the mountain, and every few minutes Alexander jumped up to admire the snow pigs in the freezer.

On a later visit, when Alexander Scott went to greet the snow pigs, he saw four pebbly eyes sitting forlornly on the ice cube tray.

It was the kind of freezer that defrosts itself.

7

A neglected orphan

MERRIDY WAS SWEEPING UP AN UNUSUAL COLLECTION of chocolate raisins. She had given the guinea pigs portions of fresh beetroot, which was a first at Green Street since beetroot was second only to brussels sprouts on her list of detested vegetables. But a generous neighbour had offered a spare swag and Merridy was not one to look at gift beets askance, so she fed them to her flock.

The guinea pigs had gobbled the beets with gusto and produced chocolate raisins of astonishing shades of pink. They appealed to Merridy's artistic sensibilities, and she vaguely wondered whether they would be good for mosaics. Perhaps she could pave the streets of Pig Heaven with purple and pink mosaic tiles, constructed with guinea pig pellets. 'If African huts have floors of stamped cow dung,' she reasoned, 'guinea pig pellets should work just as well.'

Of course Pig Heaven would not have streets as such; it would have charming walkways in front of the rows of hutches, so that she, and other attendants feeding the orphans, would keep their feet dry in bad weather.

Hazel looked at his mother sweeping, and nibbled on a personal pellet. He was enjoying the taste sensation of reconstituted beetroot.

Snow still clung to the mountain's summit. But the day was fine, with patches of sun peeking between the scurrying clouds, and Merridy needed exercise. It had been a long week editing academic garble, and her head was milling with weasel words and windbaggery and appalling constructions in passive voice.

'I want to clear my head,' she said to the guinea pigs, depositing the pellets into a spare ice cream container, just in case. 'A brisk walk should do it.'

The Doggy Beach featured a trio of Huskies and a hyperactive Maltese. The Huskies looked enchanting against the backdrop of snowy mountain, for their coats were white and their eyes as blue as the fleeting glimpses of sky. The Maltese yapped incessantly around the heels of the Huskies and Merridy thought it was lucky not to be eaten up.

Merridy passed the yacht club and strode energetically towards the Casino. Spring buds were showing on the shrubs along the esplanade lawns. She trotted across for a closer look, since she loved spring buds. Soon they would blossom into fragrant white stars, and scatter their own snowflakes across the green. Spring was one compensation for the long Tasmanian winters, she thought. The buds were wrapped tightly in glossy coats of green.

Then a rectangular object caught her eye. It sat between two distant shrubs. It looked like a hutch. One of the wheeled sort, with a wire front end and an enclosed back bedroom.

And that is how Merridy found the neglected orphan, Blackberry.

'All by himself!' she exclaimed to the guinea pig grandmother, for she had rung at once to report the discovery. 'The poor little chap!'

'There ought to be a law against it,' said her mother, which was something she had said before, but which did not make it any less important.

Merridy's cheeks were glowing, partly from the brisk air and partly from indignation. She had investigated the large padlock on the neglected orphan's hutch. His owners were security conscious, which was a good thing, thought Merridy, even in Tasmania, which was virtually crime-free. 'Yes,' she had said to the guinea pig's shiny eyes, for they were the only part of him that she could see, 'I can see they want to keep you safe, which is well-meaning and responsible. But your parents don't understand how dreadful it is,' she continued, 'to keep a single guinea pig in solitary confinement!' She thought of Nelson Mandela on Robben Island. A prison cell was a prison cell, she thought, and a dreadful fate for the undeserving.

'All I could see,' she said to her mother, 'were two shiny black eyes. He would not come out.'

'What colour is he?' asked the guinea pig grandmother. 'And how do you know he's a boy?'

'I don't,' admitted Merridy. 'But I think he's black all over, because all I could see in the bedroom were his shiny eyes.'

'Did you offer him dandelions?' asked the guinea pig grandmother, for this was a sure way to tempt out a shy guinea pig.

'I did,' said Merridy, 'and clover, and grass. But he would not come out.'

Merridy took to visiting the lonesome guinea pig whenever

she could. She talked to him gently, and wiggled treats of capsicum and carrot stick through the wire mesh of his padlocked cage. Nobody else seemed to visit him, and she wondered if he was taken indoors at night for cuddles and warmth.

'Shiny Eyes!' she would call to him. 'Shiny Eyes!' The shiny eyes watched from the depths of the bedroom. They did not come out while the guinea pig mother was visiting, but they came out and ate up her offerings when she was not.

'This is why there must be guinea pig orphanages,' declared Merridy. She was talking to Hector Protector, whom she insisted come and see the neglected orphan with the shiny eyes.

'He is probably depressed,' said Hector Protector, who was a psychologist and knew about such things. 'If he does not come out, and has no companions, he will be depressed.'

'It's a disgrace,' said Merridy, 'that depressed and neglected guinea pig orphans have nowhere to go in Tasmania.'

'Well,' said Hector Protector carefully, in case of offending the guinea pig mother's sensibilities, 'he is not strictly an orphan, because somebody keeps him in a hutch.' He did not add, 'locked up'.

Merridy huffed. 'As good as!' she said. 'I have half a mind to pignap him and bring him to Green Street. He would be much happier among my flock.'

'Yes,' said Hector Protector, wondering if he would be inveigled into illegal activities involving lock-picking and pig-snatching.

'There it is!' pointed Merridy, and trotted towards the apparently deserted hutch.

'I'm calling him Blackberry,' said Merridy to Alexander Scott. 'Because he's black and shiny.'

'Cuuu-uute!' whistled Alexander Scott. 'Are you going to

bring him to Green Street?'

'One day,' said Merridy, 'I will. When I've learned how to pick a padlock.'

'Oooh!' said Alexander Scott. 'Can I do it?'

To her flock, Merridy took to saying, 'One day, you'll have a new pig to keep you company. He's an only pig, and a depressed and shy pig. He's not used to company. And when he comes to live at Green Street, I want you to be very kind to him. He will be the Green Street Guinea Pig Orphanage's first real orphan.'

'Yes,' she would say, cuddling somepig on her fluffy green dressing gown, 'Blackberry will be our first real orphan, because you,' and she would look at the Originals, the Ridgeback Little Spot and the Guinea Buddha Choklit, 'were saved from becoming orphans in the first place by coming to live with us.'

In the event, it took the wheedles of the guinea pig grandmother on a southern visit to bring out the neglected orphan.

It was unseasonally boiling, which Merridy was pleased about because she could wear shorts, but which had caught the visitor by surprise in a surplus of winter clothing. By the time they reached Blackberry's quarters the guinea pig grandmother was sweating with heat and excitement. They crept quietly up to the hutch.

'Blackberry!' called Merridy gently.

There was no answer, but the guinea pig grandmother drew in a sharp breath. 'I can see his shiny eyes!' she said.

'Blackberry!' called Merridy again. But the shiny eyes didn't stir.

'I have protea leaves,' said the guinea pig grandmother, 'and dandelions and fresh mint.' The ancestral garden was burgeoning with spring produce and she had brought extra for the neglected orphan. She removed her gortex jacket with a puff, and brought out the bag of food.

'Blackberry!' she called in the special voice she used for the wallabies in Cataract Gorge. 'Blackberry!' She poked some mint through the wire mesh.

Merridy held her breath. There was a movement of the shiny eyes.

'Blackberry!' coaxed the guinea pig grandmother, offering a dandelion. The dandelion head got stuck in the wire mesh but the stalk hung tantalisingly just outside the bedroom doorway.

And then Merridy didn't breathe for some time.

There was a tiny scrabbling sound.

And then a black nose appeared in the doorway. It was shiny and sleek.

'Blackberry!' sang the guinea pig grandmother, as the black nose turned toward the dandelion stalk. Merridy's heart was in her mouth.

'Blackberry!' called the guinea pig grandmother, making the little kissing sounds which worked on wallabies.

And then, quietly, gingerly, shyly, Blackberry crept outside into the blast of sunshine. He was black all over and as sleek as a seal. He looked absolutely ravishing.

'Hello Blackberry!' greeted the guinea pig grandmother. 'Would you like a juicy dandelion?' Blackberry sat perfectly still, and watched her with his shiny eyes. They perched like little headlights on top of his black head.

Merridy could not utter a thing, for she was suffering a love attack which had removed her powers of speech.

'Oh!' said Merridy later, when they had returned to Green Street. 'It was a miracle!'

'You should have seen it!' she boasted to Alexander Scott, whom she had rung at once. 'Your grandmother is a genius! She's a guinea pig whisperer!'

'What's a guinea pig whisperer?' asked Alexander.

'Someone who can talk to guinea pigs and make them feel safe and relaxed,' said Merridy. 'Someone who can bring a lonely depressed only pig out into the sunshine!' Alexander imagined Blackberry with his genius grandmother whispering into his black ears.

Her mother interrupted. 'Blackberry ate three dandelions, some mint *and* a protea leaf!' she said excitedly to her grandson.

'It was a miracle!' said Merridy again.

'When are we going to pignap him?' asked Alexander Scott, who tended to go straight to the point.

'When you've learned to pick a padlock,' said Merridy, which was a silly thing to say, and for which she would one day pay a suitable penance.

8

A visit to the Top End

MERRIDY WAS PEELING AN EGG for breakfast. It was a hard-boiled free range egg. It had been boiled for twenty minutes, to make sure that it was quite hard. Merridy detested runny egg.

The guinea pig mother had a fertile dreamlife, and this morning's dreams were responsible for her hard-boiled breakfast. For long hours before she woke, Merridy dreamt she was feeding hard-boiled free range eggs to a herd of hungry guinea pigs. She had peeled the eggs carefully, and fed them to the pigs with thin, delicate strips of bacon. At the same time, Merridy had sung 'Waterloo', over and over. She had woken to 'Waterloo' and was still singing it. In her mind's eye, Choklit was still dancing on his hind legs to 'Waterloo', while she, the guinea pig mother, held his tiny front paws. 'Water-loo!' Choklit bounced, 'Da-da-da da-da-da Waterloo!' There was no accounting for dreams.

With an internal Abba concert, and an outer hard-boiled free range egg, Merridy felt enormously cheerful. The guinea pigs, of course, were hungry. But they did not eat hard-boiled eggs in the real world, or bacon. Merridy fed them guinea pig muesli in the crazy guinea pig head bowl, and weetbix. There was always a rush to see who caught the first weetbix. Choklit was first in line since he was the most devoted weetbix fan. He stood high on his hind legs and waved his nose frantically about. Chestnut, Hazel and Little Spot milled around Choklit's hind legs. Choklit snatched his weetbix and tossed it up in excitement. Choklit ate weetbix every morning but behaved as if his mother doled it out at yearly intervals. He dragged his weetbix into a corner and chomped as fast as his little mouth could chomp.

Hobart had put on another burst of summer warmth. The mountain rose grandly against a bright blue sky. There was not a speck of snow to be seen. Merridy was grateful, but nonetheless looking forward to a stint in Australia's Top End with a guaranteed dose of proper heat. She loved her visits to the Top End for it reminded her of Africa, with white thunderclouds and long golden grass and creepers of magenta bougainvillea. Hobart rarely had thunderstorms, and bougainvillea tended to wither in the cold.

'Boys!' she said. 'I'm going away. I'm going to a very hot place near the equator.' She had been telling the guinea pigs this each day for a week. She had also told Blackberry, who had listened to Merridy carefully as he watched her with his shiny headlights.

Choklit swallowed the final crumb of his weetbix and looked bereft.

'The Top End is where I buy rainbow tie-dye clothes,' said Merridy. 'I can bring you rainbow tie-dye T-shirts!' Hazel looked affronted, and his mother giggled. Hazel's golden pelt would set off a rainbow T-shirt to perfection, but Hazel disliked attire of any description, unless it was a personal sleeping bag. Merridy recalled Hazel's reaction to the pink tubular bandage. 'A triple bypass!' she exclaimed. 'What a feat that was!' Hazel gnawed on a weetbix. 'And you loathe slippers,' added Merridy. Hazel was still slipper-free, which was good for his dignity but dangerous for his ego.

'Only joking, boys!' said Merridy, and took a mouthful of hard-boiled egg. 'No T-shirts!' It was a delicious hard-boiled egg, especially on wholewheat toast.

'The Top End,' she continued, 'is a crocodile-infested place. So I'm leaving you with your grandmother. You'll be quite safe. And you'll be spoilt rotten!' Merridy finished her hard-boiled egg and began to wash up. She had guinea pig paraphernalia to pack into the fishmobile, and the black travel bag, and four boars, and her own Mr Bean suitcase, and then she would drive two hundred and seven kilometres north and deposit the boars into their guest accommodation at the ancestral household, where they would be rottenly spoilt and indulged for an entire fortnight.

The only fly in the oinkment, so to speak, was Blackberry, who was not really a fly as such, but in other respects it was an apt metaphor. For she could not take Blackberry, and so while he would be well-padlocked and as safe as houses, he would not be spoilt at all.

The Top End lacked one important thing. There were no guinea pigs.

Merridy missed her flock. She was busy, for when she was not visiting restaurants she biked along the flat Darwin bike paths and swam in the bright turquoise pools. She did not swim in the sea because of lurking crocodiles. But she felt a deep ache in the middle of her chest, and slept poorly. Being apart from her flock seemed to bring on peculiar dreams, and each morning she woke with her head full of escaping guinea pigs. In her dreams the Hazel-Houdini Effect had become contagious.

Each morning the guinea pig grandmother sent a text message to announce the latest doings of the boar quartet, which set Merridy's mind at rest, when it didn't set it to anxiety.

'Hazel wasn't in his box this morning,' said this morning's text message, which set Merridy's heart to fluttering until she read the next part, which said, 'I found him in a weetbix box with Chestnut.' Hazel had scaled the sides of his plastic sleeping quarters and squeezed into Chestnut's weetbix box, which was empty of weetbix but full of Chestnut. It had been a tight squeeze.

Bike riding built up a big sweat in the Top End, but it was very healthy. Each day Merridy went out for an early morning cycle to work off pig-related chest aches. Her favourite rest spot was on the shores of a sandy creek, where she leaned the bike up against her favourite poinciana tree and sat down under the feathery canopy. Some days little doves bobbed and cooed in the grass. Sometimes a rainbow bee-eater trilled and swooped after insects. It was a heavenly spot.

On her fifth visit to the poinciana tree Merridy's phone beeped, and beeped again.

'Hazel,' read Merridy, 'has just swallowed the opal on my pendant!' Merridy's eyes popped. 'Oh dear,' she typed with a wobbly finger, 'you'll have to inspect his chocolate raisins!'

Hazel had a weakness for pendants, and always chewed on people's necklaces if he got half a chance. He had bitten her bead necklace at the vet's and made a fearful mess. Merridy imagined her mother searching for the lost opal, and giggled. Then her chest-ache resumed with a vengeance, and a tear gathered in her eye. 'How I miss you, Hazel Baby,' she said wistfully to the poinciana.

9

A regrettable accident

AT THE SOUTHERN END OF THE CONTINENT the guinea pigs were thriving, for the ancestral household offered five-star accommodation with full room service.

The ingested opal had not affected Hazel's appetite in the slightest, and since his chocolate raisins showed no extra shine, it seemed to have disappeared for good. The guinea pig grandmother took to wearing a different, less appetising pendant.

She was a devoted pigsitter and supplied the guinea pigs with large hunks of cauliflower, cabbage, and pumpkin daily. Young Grandpa cut the guinea pigs large swathes of grass and fed them copious quantities of weeded-out weeds. Old Grandpa assisted with the weeding, and chuckled at the sight of four guinea pig mouths waiting impatiently for their next meal.

The guinea pigs ate and ate, and got fatter and fatter. They lolled about on the guest hutch lawns like miniature elephant seals. They were not used to such quantities of fodder, and were making the most of their good fortune.

Then there was an incident. Or possibly, an accident, which is not quite the same thing.

Hazel had grown too big for his blonde boots, everybody knew that. But afterwards, nobody knew who had done something about it, or whether it was done by accident or on purpose. Was it Little Spot, insistent on being top pig? Or was it Chestnut, driven to acts of desperation? Surely it wasn't Choklit, who was a gentle soul. Perhaps it was a gang attack?

Old Grandpa said, 'She's a feisty little chap. She'll be all right.' He had not yet caught up with Hazel's baubles.

Young Grandpa shook his head. 'Perhaps you should talk to an animal psychologist,' he said to the guinea pig grandmother.

The object of the mishap, the Royal Cream, had been found wounded and bleeding in the middle of the guest hutch lawn. It was a shocking spectacle, and all the more so as the usually imperturbable Hazel was trembling all over. His impeccable coat was ragged and stained, and he looked a mess. Three guinea pigs watched furtively from the upstairs bedroom.

The guinea pig grandmother managed the mishap decisively. She removed Hazel from the guest hutch lawn, and wrapped him gently in a blanket. Then she took him to the nearest vet for an expensive visit.

And afterwards, she put Hazel in a new guest hutch all by himself.

She did not say a thing to the guinea pig mother.

Alexander Scott came to investigate. He examined Hazel's wounds with enthusiasm, anticipating pocket-pet operations needing a scalpel, or at least a pocket knife. Luckily Hazel didn't need a scalpel or pocket knife. He just needed oinkment and a lot of cosseting.

Alexander Scott looked at Chestnut, Choklit and Little Spot, and they looked back at him innocently. They did not look capable of boarish behaviour requiring an animal psychologist. 'Alien abduction!' exclaimed Alexander. He looked at the innocent trio and said, 'You're lucky you didn't get abducted too!' He searched the lawn for telltale signs and evidence of crop circles, but the only crop circles had been cropped by a herd of guinea pigs, and didn't look like alien evidence.

With Hazel in solitary confinement, the atmosphere reverted to tranquillity. But everyone felt sorry for the solitary Hazel, and the guinea pig grandmother took him onto her lap at night for cuddles in front of the television. Hazel lay like a wounded emperor on his grandmother's lap, squeaking wounded squeaks as she stroked his undamaged areas and fed him special snacks. He had finally stopped trembling and was beginning to savour his convalescence.

In the morning, Hazel was treated to breakfast-on-bed. The guinea pig grandmother laid him on a special towel on her bed in the morning sunshine, and covered him up. Hazel liked being under the towel, and looked like a big grub in a cocoon. He came out periodically to eat, and stared at the guinea pig grandmother until she stroked him. If the guinea pig grandmother became too involved in her newspaper, Hazel stared until she paid him more attention. When she did so, he screamed approval, and so the guinea pig grandmother became an expert stroker.

Hazel developed a taste for bran worms. The guinea pig grandmother fed him weetbix, and human muesli, and bran worms for breakfast. Sometimes he tried to get into the bran worm box while his grandmother was involved in her newspaper.

When Hazel was completely stuffed, the guinea pig grandmother tended his wounds with oinkment and put him into his solitary hutch on the lawn. Hazel liked his solitary hutch. He popcorned and kicked his heels and ignored the other guinea pigs, who rushed up to the fence to inspect their strange-smelling and wounded companion. 'Hazel popcorns so much when he goes out in the morning,' texted the guinea pig grandmother, 'that he can hardly eat!'

It was a wonderful thought, the thought of Hazel popcorning so much that he could hardly eat. He must be very fit, thought Merridy.

Choklit missed Hazel terribly, now that his bottom was out of Hazel's reach. He gazed at his beloved through the guest hutch bars, his lower lip pouting dejectedly. Little Spot became jealous, and chased Choklit meanly into corners, and nipped him on the rear, and so Choklit was no better off than before, and possibly worse. 'Little Spot is turning into a bully!' texted the guinea pig grandmother. 'He bites Choklit on the bottom and makes him cry!' She rescued the Guinea Buddha when he cried, for she could not bear to see him weeping.

Chestnut, being neither a bully nor a target, ate until his bottom took up almost a whole pigloo.

Meanwhile the wounded emperor ignored Choklit's yearning gaze and Little Spot's proprietorial demands, and savoured his personal space and his own personal pile of weeds. Hazel was becoming accustomed to special privileges.

When the guinea pig mother returned from Darwin, she got a shock. The guinea pigs were enormous. 'They've doubled in size!' she gasped. 'They're like guinea sheep!' This was an exaggeration, fortunately, because Green Street did not accommodate sheep. The guinea sheep Chestnut leapt in fright and squeezed tightly into a pigloo.

'Where's Hazel?' asked Merridy, who was in for another shock.

The guinea pig grandmother broke the news diplomatically and in stages.

'I took Hazel to the vet,' she said, 'because he was bitten.'

Merridy looked alarmed, but before she could say 'Who did it?', the guinea pig grandmother had ducked off to fetch Hazel from his indulgence in extra bran worms. She returned with Hazel lying in her arms like a fat and furry baby, and popped a sprig of lavender between his lips. 'He's fine now,' she said calmly. 'His wounds have healed up.' And she passed the formerly pristine pedigree to his mother.

'Ohhh!' said Merridy, her breath caught in horror. She could not speak.

Merridy cradled the wounded emperor in her arms, trying to stop a tear from leaking onto her cheek. Hazel squeaked approvingly. He did not mind his battle scars. He did not even mind having one eye. It brought him a lot of attention.

'The vet gave me oinkments,' said the guinea pig grandmother. 'Wound oinkment and eye oinkment. And the wound oinkment healed his skin, but the eye oinkment didn't save his eye.'

'Oh!' lamented Merridy, finding her voice. 'My poor baby!' She stroked his love handles, which were silky and stout and full of bran. 'But you are still as beautiful as ever!'

And it was true. Hazel was more appealing than ever, even with substantial love handles and only one eye. 'You are now a battle-scarred warrior!' said Merridy. 'Hazel One-Eye, my pedigree cream boar.'

They looked at Hazel One-Eye. If anything, he seemed even larger for his boots than when he had two eyes.

'Thank you,' said Merridy to the guinea pig grandmother. 'Thank you for pigsitting the guinea pigs. And thank you for tending to Hazel's wounds. He was too overbearing, and I think somepig taught him a lesson.'

'Yes,' said the guinea pig grandmother, who had delivered the news with calm and finesse, and who deserved a medal for doing so.

Hazel One-Eye looked smugly from under his long eyelashes. He had learned how to get personal service, and it had involved personal sacrifice, but now he had his very own premises, where he could popcorn at will and ignore the wider world until he wanted something. He had organised a superior supply of bran worms, and trained his grandmother into an expert stroker.

Hazel One-Eye was immensely pleased with himself.

10

The ultimate drawcard

THE PECULIAR THING WAS that Hazel One-Eye could still throw out a look with his non-eye. His repertoire of commands had thereby expanded. With his non-eye he could toss out a reproving look, a reproachful gaze, or a hard stare. And he could throw out a good deal more with his healthy eye: approval, irritation, disapproval, disgust, bring-me-grass, stroke-my-back, where-are-my-bran-worms. It kept the guinea pig mother very busy.

Back at Green Street, the guinea pig premises needed rearranging. The pink sparkly box was brought out of retirement and became the wounded emperor's personal indoor bedroom. He could hop in and out of it at will, and stare at the other guinea pigs through the perspex tv screen. This he enjoyed, and he would taunt them with a flick of his ankles, because they were on the inside and he was a free pig. Hazel hopped for joy when he heard his mother shredding newspaper to line his personal indoor bedroom. Sometimes he was easy to please, which at least gave Merridy a break.

Downstairs, Merridy sectioned off part of the guinea pig palace. It was a lower part, with lawn and a portcullis. The portcullis allowed the battle-scarred warrior to touch noses with his neighbours, should he so desire, but it kept him safe from further mishaps. Hazel also had his own personal pigloo, in case he wanted privacy.

'The guinea pig palace,' said his mother as she adjusted his personal pigloo for easy access, 'is in perfect proportion to the dynamics of a quartet of boars – unless one of them has an extra-large ego.'

Hazel nibbled a strand of hay innocently. He was experimenting with his extra-large ego, and getting pleasing results.

The wounded emperor had quickly discovered the benefits of battle scars. It brought him sympathy, and extra massages, and numerous treats. His mother gave him breakfast-on-couch, wrapping him in a towel papoose for his greater comfort. And while he had long been the favourite of all the visitors to Green Street, now he was a veritable *piggus* celebrity. As politely as possible, Merridy fended off a sudden influx of well-wishers who offered to bind Hazel's wounds and give him recuperative cuddles. But she could only fend off so many, and then she gave up.

Hazel became an expert and appreciative recipient of extra gifts and attention, and his screams of approval were only matched by the piercing wheeks of three neglected boars begging for scraps. Hazel One-Eye had discovered the ultimate drawcard, and played it to great advantage.

Not that Choklit, Chestnut and Little Spot were really neglected. Merridy paid them as much attention as usual, but it paled beside the attentions foisted on the Angel Hazel.

Chestnut's eating had become indiscriminate, which might have been in protest, but was more likely a natural progression of his eating function. He nibbled through Merridy's mobile phone cord, which was inconvenient, and he munched the sides of the litter-tray bed, and he chewed the end of the sipper bottle in the iris-papered contraption. The sipper bottle made clunking noises when he chewed it, which kept Merridy awake at night. 'Clunk-clunk,' it went, 'clunk-clunk,' until Chestnut got bored and moved onto the wallpaper.

Chestnut also ate a hole in the striped kitchen carpet, but this was excellent, because another hole made the carpet even tattier, and soon the landlord would have to put in a new carpet. Merridy was tired of the striped carpet, and tired of asking for a new one.

Choklit watched Hazel through the perspex tv screen longingly, and Little Spot guarded the connecting doorway, now that he could, and stopped Choklit and Chestnut from moving between rooms.

Meanwhile the only pig Blackberry remained lonely on his esplanade, for his only visitor was Merridy, and she had not learned to pick a padlock yet.

'I've brought His Highness a present,' said Hector Protector one morning, squeaking the battle-scarred warrior on his knee like a fat squeaky toy. 'Would you like to see it?' Hazel squeaked approval and Merridy said, 'Yes!' She had been servicing the wounded emperor all morning, barring a quick expedition to the neglected orphan Blackberry, who remained padlocked and safe but lonely and depressed.

Downstairs, Hector Protector opened the door of his capacious ute. 'It's a Hazel-house,' he announced.

Hazel already had his own personal palace, and a pink sparkly box, and a pigloo. 'It's a Hazel-house to go in his Hazel-palace,' laughed Hector Protector.

Merridy giggled. 'I like the notice,' she said.

The Hazel-house was made from a polystyrene eski, the sort

that holds six cans of cold drink. It was white with a blue lid. The lid was strapped firmly to the rest of the eski with packaging tape. An arched doorway was cut into one end with a notice above it that read: Hazel's House – No Peeking!

'It'll be waterproof,' said Hector Protector, 'and insulating.'

'And it will suit his demands for privacy,' said Merridy, who was impressed. She put Hazel and the eski down on the lawn. 'Do you like your new house?' she asked.

Hazel looked at the eski with his good eye. It was a good-looking eski. It smelled fresh. It was very clean. But he felt suddenly obstinate, and sat unmoving, like a voluptuous cream panna-cotta in a sea of mint sauce.

Merridy and Hector Protector waited on the rickety swing seat to see what would happen. 'It's an excellent house,' said Merridy. 'Now that Hazel is a single pig, with no pig to snuggle with in nasty weather, this will keep him much warmer than a pigloo made of an ice cream tub.'

'Too much bottom-sniffing in his youth,' said Hector Protector. 'It made him a single pig!' And perhaps this was true. Hazel had been relentlessly sniffed as a piglet, and it had turned him into a nipper, and then a bully, and then there had been a mishap involving sacrifice, and he had been removed to his own personal quarters where he was very happy and could sulk and be obstinate at will. Perhaps Hazel was the only pig who didn't mind being an only pig.

Hazel, at this moment, was bored of being obstinate. The doorway into the eski was most inviting. He liked doorways and holes that led into snug caves. It suited his Houdini side. 'Oh look!' said Merridy.

Hazel squeezed through the doorway. 'Perfect fit,' said Merridy. 'By a hair's breadth!' chortled Hector Protector. Hazel popped through his doorway like a furry cork into a bottle. He was a large boar with substantial love handles, but could stretch himself narrower in times of need.

Now inside, he squeezed about to face out of the doorway. He felt comfy, and cosy, and like a lord in his brand new house. To test the going-out properties of the doorway, he squeezed himself out. 'Whoo hoo!' cheered Hector Protector.

Hazel squeezed himself back into his eski. He turned and squeezed himself back out. He did a little hop on the lawn. He squeezed himself back in, and he squeezed himself back out. He enjoyed the sensation on his love handles.

'It's a hit!' chuckled Hector Protector.

'You're a guinea pig designer architect,' said Merridy. 'I should commission you. But Hazel would be peeved. He would not like other pigs having designer eskis!'

His Highness was back in his eski-house, lying on his tummy with his perfect pink nose poking out. His nostrils were rose pink, and heart shaped, and looked adorable above his little pink mouth.

Summer was on its way, as far as a Tasmanian summer can be called 'summer'. The evenings were light and long. The mountain loomed above the city, snowless for the time being. Lawns were lush and trees in full leaf. Roses bloomed in the gardens along Green Street, and the sweet scent of honeysuckle hung in the air.

Hazel's premises continued to improve in an upmarket direction. They underwent a renovation, and acquired an extension, and then a deck. Merridy had watched certain of her acquaintances, and clearly this was the proper order of things once one passed the penniless renting stage. It was true that she was still penniless and renting, but at least she could give Hazel his own house, all to himself, and he, Hazel, need not be renting and penniless. She refused to become a slumlord, even of guinea pig apartments.

Merridy cleaned out Hazel's palace grounds and removed the ice cream bucket pigloo and certain other redundant items. She added a piece of terracotta pipe, and a terracotta pot. The pipe would make a cooling tunnel for Hazel on hot days, and the pot looked attractive.

Merridy repurposed a haul of glass bricks thrown out by the neighbours. With Hazel's eski an energy-efficient model, the rest of his property might as well follow suit. The glass bricks were insulating while letting in plenty of natural light, and so Merridy erected an annex with the glass bricks for flooring and walls. Hazel seemed pleased, and squeezed in and out of his eski and up and off his new glassed annex. When he wanted privacy he retired to his eski, and when he wanted a view or a splash of sunshine, he reclined on his glass bricks. Hazel One-Eye now had a crystal citadel.

Then Merridy added a deck, but His Highness wasn't much interested. He preferred ground floor living, and leaping onto a deck was too energetic.

But Hazel One-Eye enjoyed the dividing portcullis. He behaved like a territorial landowner and, if literate, would have erected a sign saying 'Trespassers Nipped'.

11

An important arrival

Ten days after Old Grandpa's ninety-ninth birthday, there was an important arrival. And Hazel was no longer the youngest in the family.

The new arrival was a girl, which made a change because the last five arrivals had been boys, four of them small, round and furry.

The new arrival was also small and roundish, but not as small and round as a guinea pig. She had a little bit of brownish hair, but not as much as Chestnut. She had delicate pink skin, as delicate as the Angel Hazel's, and her ears were like furled coral.

The new arrival was Alexander Scott's longed-for baby sister.

Savannah was named for the beautiful grasslands of Africa, because their memory made her mother happy and it was important to pass on the family heritage.

Alexander Scott glowed with pride. He bounced extra high on his trampoline, singing loudly. He somersaulted and back-flipped. His gymnastics were becoming spectacular and soon he would have a baby sister to bounce on the trampoline with him.

'I have a baby sister!' he shouted to the world at large. 'Her name is Savannah!'

Savannah's arrival meant that Alexander Scott and his mother had a lot to do. They had nappies to see to, and bottles to fill, and tiny socks to hang on the washing line. The rows of tiny socks twirled like so many blossoms along the twigs of the Hills Hoist.

'A baby sister is a lot of work,' said Alexander Scott to Merridy on the telephone. He was wielding a laundry basket full of miniature clothing. 'But I don't have to change her nappies!' He remembered the guinea pigs' piles of chocolate raisins with nostalgia. 'Guinea pigs are much easier to look after,' he said.

Merridy looked out of the window at the guinea pig palaces. She wondered if it was true, because her boars had given her a lot of trouble, and Hazel was a lot of work all by himself. But at least they did not have nappies.

'When are you going to pignap Blackberry?' asked Alexander Scott, who asked his hippy aunty at least once every phone call. He still had an interest in the illegal acquisition of neglected orphans, especially the lock-picking part.

'When are you going to learn lock-picking?' countered Merridy, who felt guilty that Blackberry still lived a solitary life on the esplanade. He was unlike Hazel, who enjoyed being solitary, as long as there was an audience to show off to, for being solitary required the company of others to be most enjoyed. But Hazel was not a true only pig, and that was the difference. Solitude was less agreeable, thought Merridy, if one had no alternative.

Merridy bussed up to the north of the island to visit the new arrival. This way she could make a quick visit and be back for the guinea pigs' dinner, and not have to bother about packing the fishmobile, although she still packed *padkos*. 'You will see the new baby soon,' said the guinea pig mother to her flock as she adjusted a small backpack containing a bag of sour worms, a solar-powered calculator, and a carefully wrapped parcel. Hazel was wedged into his eski, because he had been put out to grass before breakfast-on-couch and was thoroughly disgruntled. 'One day,' said Merridy to Hazel's bottom and Choklit, Chestnut and Little Spot's faces, 'Savannah will be big enough to cuddle a guinea pig, and then you'll teach her how to squeak one!' She waved cheerfully, and set off for the bus terminal.

The bus trip to Launceston took three hours, more or less, and the guinea pig mother used the time efficiently. She was calculating her budget, since it was almost a new year, and because Young Grandpa, besides being a superior swimmer, was an accountant and had taught her to budget carefully.

There was a large category of expenses relating to guinea pig husbandry. Year Three of the Guinea Pig Era had featured unexpected costs due to the arrival of two extra boars, the acquisition of a guinea pig palace, a particularly nasty collision and expensive oinkments. 'Four guinea pigs,' said Merridy, 'cost a lot more than two.' And she entered the costs of the guinea pig palace, and the black travel bag, and hay, and guinea pig muesli, and bran worms, and vegies, and the cost of a new mobile phone cord. The sun shone in through the window and powered up her special calculator. And then there are the vet bills, thought Merridy, adding in the most recent bill for Hazel One-Eye, who was an expensive pedigree with ongoing expensive maintenance fees. This was to be expected, for an expensive pedigree. Vet visits and oinkments cost a bomb. Luckily slippers were cheap.

She thought about Hazel's skin problems, which had turned out not to be skin fungus, and of his ego problems, which had turned out to be ongoing, and of all the associated oinkments.

'He has cost far more than any other pig,' she said, thinking of Choklit and Little Spot, who did not need veterinary attention, and of Chestnut, who had almost been an emergency, until the olive oil had worked.

Back at the ranch Hazel squeezed out of his eski, since his mother was not in the vicinity and could not be pointedly ignored. He popcorned a satisfied pop.

Young Grandpa, Old Grandpa and the guinea pig grandmother met Merridy at the bus station, for they were going straight away to visit the new arrival, Savannah. 'How are the grandpigs?' asked the guinea pig grandmother, and 'How is Hazel?'

'In fine fettle,' answered Merridy, 'and fortunately for next year's budget, Hazel needs no more oinkments.' She dug around in her backpack for the carefully wrapped parcel, which was suitably themed for the arrival of a very tiny guinea pig aunty with African heritage.

Young Grandpa stopped the car outside the tall red-brick two-storey house. They helped Old Grandpa out, for the seat-belt was proving obstinate, and passed him his walking stick. 'I remember,' laughed Merridy, 'when Alexander was a toddler, and he wanted his own walking stick!' It was one of her favourite photographs, the one showing her toddler nephew standing alongside Old Grandpa, with a matching walking stick which he'd found in the shrubbery. Old Grandpa chuckled. His legs weren't what they used to be, but the walking stick helped.

Savannah was a delight. Merridy's niece was silky soft, in a different way to the silky softness of a pedigree cream boar, and her eyes were large and dark with soft long lashes. She made funny little squeaks and gurgles, and Merridy stroked her tiny pink toes, which curled up because it tickled.

Alexander Scott was bursting with pride and showed his aunty the miniature clothing, and the enormous pile of nappies in the bathroom, and Savannah's bassinet which was in their mother's bedroom. 'She sleeps in here,' he said, 'so that Mum doesn't have to get up in the night to feed her!'

'That seems a very good idea,' said Merridy. She was glad she didn't have to get up in the night to feed the guinea pigs. She was also grateful for not having her bathroom stuffed with vast quantities of nappies. It was a big thing, looking after a human baby.

Then Alexander Scott helped his baby sister open her parcel. Two soft furry animals came out of the wrapping, and he crowed with glee. 'This is a *guinea pig,*' he explained to his baby sister, who was captivated by the sparkles on the discarded wrapping.

'It's to help her get in practice for the real thing,' laughed Merridy. 'After all, she's a guinea pig aunty with four guinea pig nephews already!'

The guinea pig grandmother grabbed the soft toy guinea pig, and squeezed, but it was squeakless. 'No squeaks!' she said.

The other soft toy was similar in shape to the soft toy guinea pig, but it had larger teeth and a very small tail. 'For her African heritage,' said Merridy, and her sister smiled.

'This is a *hippopotamus,*' said Alexander Scott to his baby sister, who now had a toy guinea pig on her very tiny lap. 'And I will teach you about *biltong,*' said Alexander Scott, 'and how to speak Afrikaans!' He was well-schooled in the family heritage and said to his baby sister, '*Ek is lief vir jou!*' which means, in Afrikaans, 'I love you'.

And on the bus home Merridy ruminated on her good fortune, having come all the way from Africa when she was young to the heart-shaped southern island that is Tasmania, where she had her human family, and her guinea pig family, and she felt the warmth of gratitude deep in her belly. She watched the hedgerows flit past, white with hawthorn blossoms, and she saw the purple ridges of distant mountain ranges, and the bright green of the Midlands fields, and the tall spires of poplar trees bursting into leaf, and then finally the blue hump of the mountain coming into view.

And then she walked home along the quiet streets, until she came to Green Street.

Her guinea pig family was waiting. She felt a rush of affection at the sight of four grazing forms arrayed on the green lawn, and for a minute she stood quietly at the corner of the house watching. Even Hazel looked content. The pansies were flowering in violet and mauve and beginning to cascade across the lower part of the guinea pig palace. The pots of herbs were sprouting peppermint and parsley, and the rose tree was budding pink along the falling-down shed. This was her earthly paradise, in all its humble beauty.

12

Seasonal duties

THEN SUDDENLY IT WAS CHRISTMAS.

It had been an uneventful lead-up to the festive season, which was a great relief. There had been no guinea pig woundings or natural disasters. The weather had been fine. Fine *and* sunny, which in Tasmanian weatherspeak are not the same thing.

'I brought a dandelion tree,' said Hector Protector, opening the boot of his capacious ute and hauling out a dandelion plant the size of a small eucalypt. 'They are growing into monsters in my garden, and I'm trying to get rid of them.' Merridy goggled at the huge dandelion. It had masses of juicy foliage. 'There's enough there for a pig battalion!' she said.

A loud wheeking from the guinea pig palaces drew their attention. 'Haha!' said Merridy. 'The pig battalion has spotted it!' Choklit, Chestnut and Little Spot stood in a row on their little hind legs, scrabbling the bars with their tiny front feet and wheeking frantically. 'You would think they were starved,' said Merridy, 'but they've just eaten an enormous breakfast.' The battle-scarred warrior squeezed out of his eski to inspect the ruckus. He noted the dandelion tree and bit the bars of his premises loudly, for Hazel did not stoop to wheeking for attention. The sound set Merridy's teeth on edge. 'Hazel!' she exclaimed, 'No!'

Hazel continued biting the wire, which twanged like a shockingly tuned guitar. Merridy shredded some leaves off the dandelion tree and stuffed them through the palatial bars to shut off the cacophony. It was a good Christmas present.

Merridy packed the fishmobile. Into the boot went sparkly wrapped Christmas presents, the battered Mr Bean suitcase and three ice cream bucket pigloos. In went a somewhat chewed Hazel-house. The Hazel-house now featured a custom-enlarged doorway, enlarged by the customer himself to accommodate his burgeoning love handles. And on top of the Hazel-house went a red stripy poncho in case of inclement weather.

On the back seat Merridy planted a large cardboard box with Choklit, Chestnut and Little Spot inside it. Over the box she draped a sarong, to prevent overheating. It would not do to have guinea pig heatstroke on Christmas Eve.

On the front seat Merridy stowed the supply of *padkos*: carrots for the guinea pigs, and *biltong* for herself. *Padkos* kept Merridy awake while driving, and stopped the guinea pigs from brawling.

On the floor, in front of the passenger seat, Merridy placed Hazel in the black travel bag. The travel bag now had extra holes in it, chewed by Hazel for extra air and views. These days Hazel kept the black travel bag all to himself.

Then the guinea pig mother locked the door of her eyrie, of Flat Three, and they were ready.

The fishmobile made a brief but important diversion to the esplanade. 'You will be all alone!' lamented Merridy to the shiny eyes as they dragged the dandelion branch into the bedroom. Christmas was not a good time for anyone to be alone, and it was certainly not a good thing for Blackberry. But familial duties called, and so Merridy reluctantly left the neglected orphan to his lonely and unfestive season, vowing once again to rescue him from his misfortune and bring him to Pig Heaven, as soon as she possibly could.

The roads were quiet, and the sun shone on the still-green hills along the Midlands Highway. Hazel gruntled gently in his black travel bag. It was a new sound, this Hazel-gruntling, for Hazel was becoming a deeply contented pig, at least in spells. Today he was enjoying a spell of travelling contentment, complete with *padkos.*

The ancestral household was in an uproar.

Alexander Scott erupted from the front door, wearing a Christmas hat. He looked like a bright-eyed Christmas elf. Close on his heels came the guinea pig grandmother, with a bunch of lavender in one hand and a sheaf of dandelions in the other.

'Wheek wheek!' squeaked Merridy's elfin nephew, popcorning like a jack-in-a-box. 'Wheek wheek!' squeaked the guinea pig grandmother, giving her daughter a lavender-scented hug. 'Wheek wheek!' squeaked Merridy, opening the back door of the fishmobile. 'Wheek wheek!' shrieked the guinea pigs, falling about at the sight of fodder. Except for Hazel One-Eye, who sat fatly in his black travel bag and pretended to ignore the din. The fodder would come to him in good time.

'Hello,' said a voice from behind. It was the voice of Young Grandpa, who held a wad of long grass and his grass clippers. He did not speak guineaspeak.

'Welcome,' said Young Grandpa, unleashing a flood of English. 'Welcome!' cried the guinea pig grandmother, embracing Merridy once more. 'Pleeeeease help me make the trifle!' begged

Alexander, wrapping himself round his aunty's middle. 'Where's Hazel?' exclaimed the guinea pig grandmother. 'Has he grown any bigger?' 'Pleeeeease,' wheedled Alexander Scott. Merridy struggled to stay upright for her nephew was very heavy around her middle. 'In his travel bag,' and 'Yes Alexander!' and 'No Alexander!' and 'Alexander, get off!' cried the guinea pig mother, her knees buckling.

It was going to be a noisy Christmas.

Christmas Eve dinner was the usual magnificent feast. The human contingent ate a great deal of roast turkey, with roast potatoes and vegetables and an enormous ham and a gallon of turkey gravy. Only Old Grandpa didn't eat the turkey gravy, because Old Grandpa didn't like gravy, or broccoli, or cream. Old Grandpa doused his roast turkey in a white blizzard, which overflowed onto the Christmas tablecloth. But at his age, which was less than one year short of a century, he could afford to eat a great deal of salt.

The guinea pig contingent ate the guest hutch grass rapidly down to a pseudo-marsupial lawn. It was flavoured with white lawn daisies.

Alexander's uncle was absent. He was trotting the globe, and currently in Brazil, surfing and chasing a Brazilian lady with excellent buttocks. With no uncle to wrestle, Alexander wrestled his gymnastical mother and Young Grandpa.

Merridy stayed sitting to avoid being wrestled. She sat next to Old Grandpa, and they read bad jokes from Christmas crackers. Old Grandpa didn't feel like wrestling either, although he had been a keen boxer in his youth. 'I was a featherweight,' said Old Grandpa. 'It was in Johannesburg,' he said. 'In winter it was so cold I slept with my feet in my socks up the sleeves of my overcoat.'

'Gosh,' said Merridy, 'that sounds colder than Tasmania!'

The guinea pig grandmother appeared bearing a heavyweight trifle. It almost overflowed from the great crystal bowl. Spirals of Swiss roll could be seen through the glass, and blobs of red jelly. It was the work of Alexander and his aunty, which is to say, artistry crossed with reckless abandon. It was topped with a snow-covered landscape, which was lumpish, since Alexander had recklessly whipped the cream almost to butter. But it had red cherry decor, and silver baubles, and a tiny fir tree, and a diminutive plastic robin redbreast, and looked a Christmassy landscape nonetheless.

'Watch out for the money!' hollered Alexander, who had hidden fifty cent pieces in the custard. 'Don't break your teeth, Old Grandpa!' And he cackled naughtily. Old Grandpa giggled. His teeth were unbreakable, because they were false teeth.

The new baby Savannah slept deeply in her capsule under the Christmas tree. She looked like an adorable and tiny angel with her flawless soft skin and her tiny soft curls.

Hazel was put out. The commotion had been satisfying to begin with, indicating the arrival of dandelions and other gourmet treats from the ancestral garden. He had gnawed a twig of scented geranium and guzzled a long sprig of mint and masticated a spray of confetti bush with a tantalising lemon fragrance. It had been a pleasing degustation of festive flavours, but now he was impatient. The lavender offering had long since disappeared, and so had the dandelions, and his patch of guest hutch lawn was mown as flat as the Nullarbor. Choklit had gone to sleep beneath the next-door ramp, and Little Spot lay comatose on the landing, and Chestnut had gone to ground in the hay. There was no entertainment to be had, for there was no pig to be bullied or ignored, and no human to offer cosseting and admiration.

Hazel stared crossly at the ancestral household but his come-out-at-once-with-bran-worms look failed to elicit a single willing human.

The humans were gathered around the new Christmas angel. They had worked off their festive energy, and were lying in various sluggish positions on the carpet like a collection of overfed warthogs, except for Old Grandpa who sat in his chair reading a hefty novel. Old Grandpa stayed as thin as a whistle, because he never over-ate, even at Christmas.

The humans had completely forgotten the Angel Hazel, who had manifested his Christmas baubles one year earlier and proven his status as a well-endowed pedigree cream boar. Instead they encircled the Angel Savannah, who had woken up. They were admiring her uncreased forehead and her tiny pink hands. Savannah gazed at her human family with bemusement, for they were wearing unusual headdresses with enchanting twinkles, and one of them had a Christmas bauble in his mouth.

Alexander spat out the Christmas bauble, which had come off the tree and was a vivid shade of lilac. Savannah opened her mouth wide and her eyes crinkled and she showed her cute pink gums. But before Merridy could congratulate her nephew on making his baby sister smile, she felt a sharp twinge. It felt like indigestion but with shades of guilt. 'Ooof!' she grunted, heaving herself up on her arms and peering out of the window. She could make out three slumbering forms in the main guest hutch, and a solitary form in the guest hutch annex. Hazel was slumped beside his eski with a distinctly dejected air. Merridy squinted, for she was not used to Hazel looking dejected, and thought it must be a mistake, but it was not.

And so the Emperor Hazel added another ruse to his box of tricks. It involved hunching on the for'ard side, and sagging in the stern, and a drooping of the lower lip. It was the perfect posture to gain instant consideration, and Merridy stumbled out of the front door as fast as her legs would carry her. For it was a piteous sight, the sight of the Emperor Hazel looking dejected, and she was reminded that underneath all that love handle he was still her tiny-weeny cream boar.

And so Christmas Eve ended satisfactorily, with the Emperor Hazel perched upon the new Christmas angel's tummy, where he was dribbled on; and then upon Old Grandpa's trousers, where he was soothingly stroked; and then inside Alexander Scott's shirt, where he snoozed snugly; and then on Alexander's mother's kneecap where he was tickled; and then upside down on the guinea pig grandmother's lap where he was fed weeds collected by Young Grandpa on a garden excursion; and finally, on his mother's chest, where he gruntled into her neck as she sang him his special Hazel song. 'Hazel, Hazel, gimme your answer do-o-o-o…' Hazel enjoyed the lullaby and warbled tunefully under his mother's chin. 'I'm amazled… all for the love of you-o-o-o.' It was a fitting end to a moderately pleasant day in the life of His Highness Hazel One-Eye, and he closed his good eye with contentment, and left his funny eye open just in case.

13

Festive indignities

CHRISTMAS MORNING DAWNED FINE AND SUNNY, which in Tasmanian terms is a double-win. Merridy quickly donned her favourite shorts and peeked out of the living room window. Three pigs were still in bed, but Chestnut was out eating the remains of the pseudo-marsupial lawn. It was hard to believe it was the Angel Hazel and the Cherub Chestnut's second Christmas already.

Merridy skipped into the kitchen, where there was the usual leftover trifle for breakfast. She picked muesli instead, and left the leftovers to those with stronger early morning stomachs. 'Happy Christmas!' she said to Young Grandpa, who was eating leftover trifle. 'Happy Christmas, Old Grandpa,' she said to Old Grandpa, who had long finished his toast and marmalade and was onto the washing up.

As Merridy finished her meal, the guinea pig grandmother burst out of the bedroom. She was still in her dressing gown, which trailed bits of sparkly paper and Christmas ribbon. 'Merridy!' she said, 'We must dress up the guinea pigs!'

Merridy swallowed a final cherry, and spat out the pip. She followed her mother into the garden.

Hazel was nowhere to be seen. Or more accurately, only a patch of cream-coloured rump could be seen in his eski-house doorway. Hazel had wedged himself as far into his eski as his love handles would allow.

The dressing up passed the time until Alexander, the new Christmas angel and their mother turned up and everyone could open their presents. Merridy photographed Chestnut draped in tinsel, and Little Spot poking out of a party hat like a guinea pig ice cream in an ice cream cone. The guinea pig grandmother dressed Choklit in reindeer horns, and put Savannah's Christmas bib on Hazel's back like a scarlet cape. Then she put a pointed party hat on Hazel's head. 'He looks remarkably like a medieval maiden,' said Merridy. Hazel chewed a hole right through his party hat.

And then it was time. Under the Christmas tree sat Young Grandpa. He sat next to the piles of gleaming presents. Young Grandpa was Master of Ceremonies.

Everyone else sat in a big circle. They sat on the couches and on the carpet, and Old Grandpa sat in his armchair reading *The Saints of Christmas Past* and stroking the heads of two small furry saints absent-mindedly. Savannah slept deeply in her baby capsule.

Young Grandpa turned to the piles of gleaming presents, ready to choose the first one. He was looking for one labelled 'Alexander Scott' since Alexander was the most impatient. 'What's this?' he said, looking at a large mound of chocolate raisins.

The furry saint Hazel looked as innocent as a brand new foal. 'Oh dear,' said Merridy. 'Those are Hazel-presents.'

Alexander Scott screeched with mirth. 'How can you tell?' he demanded. 'Maybe they're Choklit-presents!'

'I'm afraid,' said Merridy, 'that the size gives them away. Hazel's are the biggest.'

'Those,' said Young Grandpa, 'are *not* the sort of presents we are opening this morning.' He went to fetch the dustpan, for chocolate raisins on the carpet needed sweeping up.

The present-opening was a roaring success. Young Grandpa presided over the chaos with admirable calm, dispensing presents at timely intervals. Old Grandpa received a whole canister of chocolate raisins, which were fortunately not a gift from Hazel.

There was a parcel from Brazil which caused great excitement. It was from Alexander's uncle, and it contained a good deal of Brazilian chocolate and a dvd, but no buttocks. Everyone gathered round the computer, but it was a matter of time and error before the dvd showed up on Young Grandpa's computer screen. 'Let me do it!' said Alexander. But Young Grandpa had already done it, by accident if not design, and the film began to roll.

'Galloping Galloways!' grunted Merridy, amid exclamations of admiration (Alexander) and horror (the guinea pig grandmother). Young Grandpa said, 'Watch out for excellent buttocks.'

In the event, there were no buttocks. Alexander's uncle had paid a large amount of money to fly up in a small aeroplane and come down via an even smaller parachute. He had flown up above Rio de Janeiro, and plummeted down towards Copacabana beach. He had screamed loudly during the plummet, and the entire process had been filmed at close quarters. The onlookers were amazed at the size of his screaming mouth. It made for gripping entertainment. The guinea pig grandmother was spared absolute trauma by the thought that her pride and joy had survived in sufficiently good condition to post the dvd in time for Christmas, and so must have come to a happy landing.

Which he had. The parachute opened on cue, and Alexander's uncle stopped screaming. He floated in heavenly circles above Christ the Redeemer, the cliff-clinging *favelas*, and toward the strip of white sand speckled with a thousand sunbathers. The onlookers waited for the bird's eye view of two thousand sunbathing buttocks, excellent or otherwise, but the parachute veered off toward a line of skyscrapers, and then the film ran out.

That night Merridy dreamed of a vast golden entity circling above Rio de Janiero. It was harnessed with a scarlet harness, and a scarlet cape flew up behind it. The scarlet harness hung from a silken parachute, and the golden being floated effortlessly over Christ the Redeemer, and high above a series of winding peninsulas and turquoise bays edged with glittering white and shoals of tiny yachts, their sails flickering like a thousand butterfly wings. A tiny human sat upon the neckline of its scarlet cape, and she could have sworn it was her brother, but her eyes were blurry, and she could not make him out. Then the creature loosed a golden egg onto Sugarloaf mountain, and blinked one enormous eye. Merridy stirred restlessly as the great eye found her. It flashed out across the oceans of the world and found her in her bed. She cried out, cowering into her pillows, for she suddenly saw that the great eye belonged to a Great Pig in the Sky, and he was solid gold and terrible.

But then the great eye blinked benignly beneath its long dark lashes, and winked.

14

Hazel's earthly kingdom

AND THAT IS HOW THE WOUNDED EMPEROR, the Emperor Hazel One-Eye, the Royal Cream, established himself as Lord and Master of an earthly kingdom on the heart-shaped island that is Tasmania. It was a modest kingdom, with swards of verdant green and various suitable accommodations, and a selection of human minions and inferior guinea pigs, but His Highness Hazel was very pleased with it, for the time being.

And that is the story of the tiny-weeny androgynous and virginal angel who became a magnificent and obviously male specimen of the genus *guinea piggus domesticus*, director of a quartet of boars, top top pig, and with a human mother increasingly under the sway of his personal demands.

And so the human mother, the guinea pig mother Merridy, found herself for no explicable reason fiddling with the new social media device called Facebook, which she had joined solely to follow the adventures of her absent brother, who was reclining on Copacabana beach among a gazillion spectacular

Brazilian derrieres at that very moment. Her brother closed his eyes against the sun, since the gleaming sea of buttocks was somewhat overwhelming, if most appetising, at the precise instant that Merridy uploaded a profile photograph of a large blonde guinea pig. He opened his eyes again to view the smorgasbord of Brazilian flesh as his sister typed in 'His Highness Hazel'. He settled his back onto the sun-hot sand as she argued with her motherly principles, for Merridy did not believe in displays of favouritism and insisted on treating her children equally, except for Hazel, but that was to make up for his woundedness, and his isolation in separate quarters, for no pig is an island, and she did not want him becoming dejected, and so she was not really displaying favouritism at all.

This Merridy told herself as the blonde guinea pig gazed at her from the screen with his good eye, which was his beautiful eye, and his all-too-knowing eye. She did not know that Hazel One-Eye's ego was still inflating, and that a personal Facebook page would lead to a personal and global Fan Club, and demands for *piggus* literature, and a whole lot more besides.

But who could blame her? It was difficult not to cosset a wounded emperor with long eyelashes and perfect pink lips, and Hazel had cast his cosseting spell on all and sundry, and was working on Young Grandpa, who did not yet cosset but supplied a good quantity of weeds.

And perhaps it was an extension of the spell which had enchanted the guinea pig mother at that long-ago Hobart Guinea Pig Show, when she had adopted a diminutive but expensive pedigree and a cheap but handsome mongrel, and changed her life forever.

Merridy guiltily closed the Apple laptop and glanced at the perspex tv screen, which was featuring a *piggus* version of *Big Brother*, with Little Spot playing spy and Choklit and Chestnut fighting over a motley scrap of household equipment. In the pink sparkly box beside, His Highness Hazel rested on a royal cushion of shredded newspaper topped with hay, speculatively chewing. His fur was still blonde and lustrous, and his rose-petal ears were still delicate and pink, and he was definitely used to adulation.

That night, which was the eve of a New Year, the fourth year of the Guinea Pig Era, Merridy lay beneath her window under a canopy of silver moonlight. She dreamed once more of Pig Heaven, and this time the hutches were twined with climbing nasturtiums. She trod barefoot among the summer grasses, picking a scarlet flower and savouring the sharp peppery tang. She plucked another and offered it to a newly arrived orphan, who was orange and plump and flashed a bright white star on his forehead. The new arrival wheeked in consternation, for he did not eat nasturtiums, and was thoroughly alarmed by the unfamiliar offering. And so Merridy lifted him up, and he lay fat and sleek in her bare arms, and she crooned a little crooning song which said he was an orphan no more, and would live out his days in peace among the pigs of Green Street.

Then her dream turned the colour of copper, as if the African sun had burned away the world to heat and light. She held the white-starred guinea pig to her breast, and closed her eyes, surrendered to the heat beating bronze against her eyelids, burning gold upon her skin. She was at the centre of a great heart, and her own heart pulsed in synchrony, and so did the tiny heart pressed against her. And then she felt only the beating, and the beating, of the great heart, which was her heart, and the guinea pig's heart, and the heart of all things.

In the morning light, which was early, it being midsummer, Merridy woke. She could remember a white-starred guinea pig; she could still feel his sleek plump body in her hands. And there had been something golden and warm and terribly important, but that she had forgotten. She felt bereft.

She peeped over the sill to check the mountain for weather. It was calm and still, with a pale sky promising blue. A perfect summer's day.

But all through breakfast her heart ached with a deep longing. Her mind reached after wisps of dream-memory, but they were diaphanous mists which retreated with each act of focus. She muddled up the breakfasts, scattering human muesli into the iris-papered contraption and giving three weetbix to Hazel, who was piqued not to be fed on-couch as he deserved, but who accepted the extra weetbix with alacrity, for he deserved that too.

It was with some relief that Merridy answered the ringing telephone, for her brain was becoming boggled and fractious. 'Wheek wheek!' squeaked a familiar voice. It was the voice of Alexander Scott. 'When are we going to pignap Blackberry?!'

'Have you learned to pick a padlock?' returned his aunty, whose ethical reservations about lock-picking still conflicted with a powerfully ethical urge to pignap neglected orphans.

'I have!' cackled Alexander Scott. 'I know how to do it!' Merridy could hear a strange whittling sound, and then realised it was not her nephew, but Chestnut gnawing on his woodchip doorway. 'No!' she said to Chestnut, and 'Yes!' shouted Alexander Scott. 'We are going to pignap Blackberry!'

The last day

FOR FORTY DAYS AND NIGHTS Merridy had been hounded by a relentless and insistent muse in the form of a golden guinea pig.

She was exhausted beyond words, and wordless beyond exhaustion. This did not stop the Royal Boar from prodding at his mother until she burped out a few final paragraphs. *Pig Tails* was rapidly approaching completion, and the Time was Now.

And so Hazel completed the first-ever guinea pig novel, and he was pleased with what he saw. He saw his mother splayed across the kitchen table with her eyes closed and her breath even and slow, for she was sleeping the sleep of the living dead. He saw his *magnum piggus* on the laptop screen, and it was making excellent progress. He saw three guinea pigs snoozing in their sleeping boxes, and one with a ginger crown perched upon a cardboard throne.

Hazel saw the sun sparkling off the River Derwent, and the mountain stark against the blue summer sky. He saw a puffed cloud linger on the mountain crest. Hazel was pleased with his earthly paradise, and pleased with his island kingdom, and pleased with his literary achievement.

'Where will it be published?' asked the guinea pig grandmother.

'I'm sure His Highness will see to *that*,' said Merridy, who hadn't the foggiest.

'Since it's the first-ever guinea pig novel,' said Alexander Scott, who was to blame for introducing Merridy to guinea pigs in the first place, 'it should go in the *Guinea* Book of Records!' Alexander Scott was now a strapping youth and held a sister on each knee.

Everybody laughed.

'But,' said the guinea pig grandmother plaintively, 'you haven't told us about Bluebell.' Merridy's mother had been very fond of Bluebell.

'I remember Bluebell,' said Savannah. 'He was from the police force!'

'I remember Bluebell!' echoed Ebony. 'He had long hair!'

'And Bramble!' added the guinea pig grandmother. 'What about Bramble Blackbelt?'

'Chickpea!' shouted Ebony. 'Chickpea was my favourite.'

'And Jupiter!' said Savannah. 'Jupiter the Gymnastical Ginger Ninja!'

Young Grandpa diverted the conversation to practicalities. 'It's time Hazel One-Eye earned you some money,' he said.

'I couldn't agree more,' said the world's first guinea pig novelist. 'It's exhausting channelling a voracious Pig God, and I deserve a well-paid rest!'

'Besides which,' she said, 'I deserve a great deal of chocolate. Which I will need as brainfood for Books Two and Three of *The Guinea Pig Trilogy*.'

Merridy winced. His Highness Hazel had great expectations

and had just channelled his mother an important message. 'Oh no!' she moaned. 'A trilogy!'

And so Hazel begat *The Guinea Pig Trilogy*, which began with the first-ever guinea pig novel, *Pig Tails*, the first novel in earthly history to be written for a guinea pig, about a guinea pig, and by a guinea pig. It began with Hazel One-Eye's consummate vanity and ended with his satisfactory elevation to furry celebrity. It launched his mother onto a path of fame and fortune culminating in a cavy movement of cosmic proportions. And it raised a new consciousness on the part of humanity, for never again was a guinea pig schnitzeled, kebabed or presented as a crisp whole roast with a chilli in its mouth.

His Highness Hazel Rules OK.
Blessings to his acolytes.

A GLOSSARY of *piggus* terms

alter piggo – a guinea pig's *alter ego* or *doppelganger*

baubles – essential male apparatus

bareback riding – see *humping* and *rodeo*

boar – the guinea pig male, featuring baubles and dominance behaviour

bottom pig – the guinea pig at the bottom of the pecking order

bottom-throw – a sideways toss of the rump to show dominance

bran worms – a fibre-rich breakfast cereal for humans and the most important words in Hazel's vocabulary, besides *weetbix*

caboose – the last guinea pig in a *piggy train*

capybara – a large but inferior relative of the guinea pig

cavia porcellus – the Latin name for *guinea pig*

caveat emptor – buyer beware: a poorly spelled Latin term warning the potential cavy purchaser that her purchase may have life-changing consequences

cavy – another name for *guinea pig*

chocolate raisin – the neat package of excreta from a guinea pig, so-called because of its resemblance to a popular human confection

copraphagy – technical term for ingestion of *personal pellets*; this balances the gut flora and keeps digestion healthy

conga line – see *piggy train*

crest – a rosette formation on the forehead which may resemble a crown or wig

dominance behaviour – used to establish the pecking order, including *humping*, *rumblestrutting*, *face-offs* and *bottom-throwing*

drama-pig – guinea pig *prima donna*; displays excessive shows of emotion for effect

engine – the lead guinea pig in a *piggy train*

face-off – dominance contest in which the guinea pig with the highest nose wins

HHH – His Highness Hazel

hamsters – very small, much inferior rodents, often confused with guinea pigs

hamster wheel – an exercise device unsuitable for guinea pigs

gruntling – unusual guinea pig vocalisation indicating supreme contentment

guinea pig – small, appealing rodent with rounded body and twiddly legs; originally from Peru

guinea pig muesli – a mix of dried grains, vegetables and fruit bits

guinea pig tv – live reality tv in the home, commonly featuring *Game of Thrones*

guinea piggus domesticus – pseudo-Latin name for the species *cavia porcellus*

guineaspeak – guinea pig language consisting of multiple vocalisations (wheeks, shrieks, chirps, twitters, rumbles, growls and gruntles)

humping – dominance behaviour where one guinea pig jumps onto another guinea pig's back, flank, or head, and the rest can be left to your imagination

king pig – the top pig

magnum piggus – you're reading it

mongrel – of mixed breeding

only pig – single guinea pig living without company of its own kind

pecking order – guinea pig social hierarchy

pedigree – purebred

pellet – see *chocolate raisin*

personal pellet – *chocolate raisin* excreted by a guinea pig for its own consumption

piggy train – a line-up of humping guinea pigs with fast locomotion

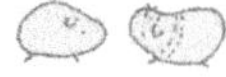

Pig God – supreme being with a difficult temperament and a gluttonous ego; see HHH

piggus – see *guinea pig*

pigloo – small rounded guinea pig shelter, with entry doorway or tunnel

pocket pet – common descriptor of pocket-sized pets like mice, rabbits, hamsters and of course, guinea pigs

popcorning – when a guinea pig jumps or hops in the air with elation

portcullis – a peace-keeping device placed between badly behaved guinea pigs

proper flora – guinea pig gut bacteria, kept in balance by the practice of *copraphagy*

pseudo-marsupial lawn – grass browsed to a smooth flat plain by non-marsupials like *guinea pigs*

rodeo – a continuing display of humping, with the humper and humpee taking turns at *bareback riding*

rosette – a whorl of fur with a tiny bald spot in the middle

rumblestrutting – rumbling vocalisation involving vibration of the torso and waggling of the bottom from side to side, to show dominance

top pig – the guinea pig at the top of the pecking order

weetbix – a breakfast cereal biscuit for humans which ought not to be fed to guinea pigs (but if you'd like to try some yourself, look for Weet-Bix, Weetabix or Vitabrits)

wheeking – onomatopoeic term for guinea pig squeaks

An important note about guinea pigs

Guinea pigs are intelligent, social, deeply affectionate, and despite their solid appearance, rather fragile. They need gentle care and plenty of attention.

To hold a guinea pig, use both hands, with one hand beneath the rump for safety and the other behind the back or neck. Let the guinea pig sit against your chest or on your lap.

To squeeze or massage a guinea pig, use one or both hands, and find the ticklish spots by gently rubbing and scratching. Some guinea pigs like to be massaged behind the head, some beneath the chin, some on the tummy, and some in the armpits. If the guinea pig nips, that means 'please do something else'.

To put a guinea pig down, use both hands and place the guinea pig rump first on the ground. This will stop the guinea pig jumping out of your hands and hurting itself.

To catch a guinea pig, approach quietly and use both hands gently. This requires patience but as a guinea pig comes to trust you it will allow you to catch it sooner (unless it is playing chases). You can herd the guinea pig into a corner or container to make catching easier. Although characters in this book are said to tackle guinea pigs to the ground, this is not the proper way to catch a guinea pig!

Weetbix, human muesli and bran worms are not recommended guinea pig food. The guinea pig mother didn't know this when she first got guinea pigs, and they became rather fat, especially Hazel One-Eye because he ate the most bran worms. It is best to feed guinea pigs grass hay, fresh grass, fresh vegies, some fresh fruits, and pellets recommended by your vet. But no potatoes, onions or iceberg lettuce.

The Proper Care of Guinea Pigs is a real book, by Peter Gurney, and it tells you how to look after guinea pigs properly. There are tons of other manuals and useful websites about guinea pig care, and when the guinea pig mother was learning to be a responsible parent, she used plenty.

Watership Down is also a real book, by Richard Adams. It has no guinea pigs in it, but if you haven't read it yet, that is a serious omission. It's a famous animal story about rabbits, with a valiant boy-rabbit hero called Hazel. Luckily the one-eyed Pig God doesn't realise he was named after an inferior, burrowing rodent with ridiculously long ears.

Grateful thanks...

To **Corrianne**, for inspiration from far-off Brazil which started me writing the first draft of *Pig Tails* for National Novel Writing Month 2010. What can I say – you got me into this!

To **Janet**, for letting Alex have two guinea pigs, and to **Alex**, for choosing Choklit and Little Spot. You got me into this too!

To **Peter M**, for coming to the Hobart Guinea Pig Show and for not stopping me buying Hazel and Chestnut. I suspect it's your fault as well.

To **Mum** and **Dad**, for pigsitting the grandpigs and putting up with rambling guest accommodations, hay on the carpet, and the occasional escaped chocolate raisin. I thank you for encouraging me to read, write, photograph and draw as a child. This fed my desire to make books like this one.

To various **family members**, for allowing your names and characters to be misused in the services of a one-eyed Pig God.

To **Jonathan** for registering guineapigempire.com for me all those years ago and for steady encouragement.

To **Mark**, for your love, enthusiasm and understanding, and for adopting my furry babies.

To **Annette**, for your piggy knowledge and dedication to guinea pig welfare.

To the **Facebook Pig Tails fan club** for cheering me on as I posted the original unedited chapters online (which for an editor is a supreme display of insanity).

To **many persons in Tassie and worldwide** for encouragement, for enjoying my guinea pigs in person or virtually, and waiting patiently for the appearance of this book.

To those who read the final draft and gave valuable feedback: **Mark**, **Mum**, **Kaye**, and **Noelle**.

To **Tom** and **Marilyn**, for the homegrown organic carrots.

To my editor **Sharon Moore**, for your good humour, appreciation, and eye for detail.

To **Kylie**, for your self-publishing expertise.

To **my guinea pigs**, my squeaky boys, my furry gurus. You have given me so much.

And to **Hazel One-Eye**, my soul pig. *Namaste.*

The authors

THERE IS SOME DISPUTE as to the real author of this book. Merridy thinks she wrote it and cheekily put her name on the front, but Hazel thinks he wrote it and is sulking fit to cause a thunderstorm.

Perhaps it was an interspecies-interdimensional collaboration, in which case, let the quantum scientists work that out.

Photograph courtesy of Peter Morse © 2006